P9-DFY-393

Christmas came once a year.

And this year Maggie would embrace it. Trees, sledding, cookies. She was all in.

As if he read her mind, her son asked, "Can you come and help us pick out a tree, Finn?"

"I don't know if you heard," Finn said, "but I'm the best tree hunter in all of Alaska." To which her boy's face lit up with excitement.

There was no doubt about it. Oliver was blooming right before her eyes. And it had everything to do with Finn. She should know. He'd done the same for her when she was a child.

She told Finn when her son scampered off. Then warned, "I'm just worried he might get too attached to you. Oliver isn't looking for a father figure. He's looking for a father."

"No worries, Mags. We're buddies," Finn assured her. "Surely that can't be a bad thing."

"No, that's not a bad thing." Not for her son, she thought. But what about her? Was being Finn's buddy enough?

Belle Calhoune grew up in a small town in Massachusetts. Married to her college sweetheart, she is raising two lovely daughters in Connecticut. A dog lover, she has one mini poodle and a chocolate Lab. Writing for the Love Inspired line is a dream come true. Working at home in her pajamas is one of the best perks of the job. Belle enjoys summers in Cape Cod, traveling and reading.

Books by Belle Calhoune

Love Inspired

Alaskan Grooms

An Alaskan Wedding
Alaskan Reunion
A Match Made in Alaska
Reunited at Christmas
His Secret Alaskan Heiress
An Alaskan Christmas

Reunited with the Sheriff
Forever Her Hero
Heart of a Soldier

An Alaskan Christmas

Belle Calhoune

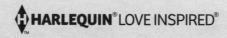

If you purchased this book without a cover you should be aware that this book is stolen property. It was reported as "unsold and destroyed" to the publisher, and neither the author nor the publisher has received any payment for this "stripped book."

Recycling programs
for this product may
not exist in your area.

® LOVE INSPIRED BOOKS

ISBN-13: 978-0-373-62304-4

An Alaskan Christmas

Copyright © 2017 by Sandra Calhoune

All rights reserved. Except for use in any review, the reproduction or utilization of this work in whole or in part in any form by any electronic, mechanical or other means, now known or hereinafter invented, including xerography, photocopying and recording, or in any information storage or retrieval system, is forbidden without the written permission of the editorial office, Love Inspired Books, 195 Broadway, New York, NY 10007 U.S.A.

This is a work of fiction. Names, characters, places and incidents are either the product of the author's imagination or are used fictitiously, and any resemblance to actual persons, living or dead, business establishments, events or locales is entirely coincidental.

This edition published by arrangement with Love Inspired Books.

® and TM are trademarks of Love Inspired Books, used under license. Trademarks indicated with ® are registered in the United States Patent and Trademark Office, the Canadian Intellectual Property Office and in other countries.

www.Harlequin.com

Printed in U.S.A.

But they that wait upon the Lord
shall renew their strength;
they shall mount up with wings as eagles;
they shall run, and not be weary;
and they shall walk, and not faint.
—*Isaiah* 40:31

For my brother, Stephen.
For introducing me to Steinbeck
and *East of Eden*, a book that changed my life.

Acknowledgments:

For all the readers who have enjoyed the
Alaskan Grooms series and asked for more.

For editors Emily Rodmell and Giselle Regus, for
all their hard work and dedication on this project.

Chapter One

Finn O'Rourke paced back and forth in terminal 27A of the Anchorage airport. He looked around him, noticing the pine wreaths and red ribbons adorning the walls. The Christmas decorations provided a dose of holiday cheer. For the most part, airports were pretty stark places. He took a quick glance at his watch. His passengers should have met him here twenty minutes ago so he could fly them on the last leg of their journey to his hometown of Love, Alaska. A grumbling noise emanated from his stomach, and he knew it had nothing to do with hunger pains. Butterflies had been fluttering around in his belly ever since he landed in Anchorage. He didn't know why he felt so nervous.

Perhaps it had something to do with his client, Maggie Richards. Twenty years stood between himself and Maggie. A lifetime really. She was a mother now with a small child she was raising alone.

She'd hired his brother's company, O'Rourke Charters, and now he was flying her back to Love, where she would begin her new life, courtesy of her uncle, Tobias.

Tobias Richards. He was the reason Maggie and her son were relocating to Alaska from Massachusetts. There was nothing like an inheritance to turn a person's world upside down, Finn thought. Tobias had gone to glory with a few surprises up his sleeve. Finn had just found out he had also been named in Tobias's will. Receiving the paperwork last evening had been a mind-blowing experience.

Finn felt a twinge of sadness at the realization that his good friend was gone. He missed him terribly. Tobias had been one of the few people who'd truly understood Finn. And he'd gone out of his way to help him on multiple occasions. In fact, he was still aiding him from beyond the grave.

Finn let out a deep breath. After all these years he was going to come face-to-face with Tobias's niece, Maggie, his childhood friend. They had been as thick as thieves during her visits to Love when they were kids. Ancient history, he reminded himself. She probably wouldn't even remember him.

He grinned as memories of catching salamanders and skating at Deer Run Lake washed over him like a warm spring rain. They had shared secrets and explored caves and promised to be best friends forever. His friendship with Maggie had been special, and it had come to an abrupt end mere months before his entire childhood imploded. Perhaps it was the reason why those memories were engraved on his heart like a permanent tattoo.

All of a sudden a woman came walking toward

terminal 27A with a small child in tow. She had dark hair and appeared to be struggling with a large-sized piece of luggage. Her tiny companion was dragging a rather large duffel bag behind him. A feeling of familiarity washed over Finn at the sight of her. As she came closer, there was no doubt in Finn's mind about her identity. It was Maggie!

Little Maggie Richards had matured into a beautiful woman, Finn realized. Despite the fact that he hadn't seen her in twenty years, Finn would have recognized her anywhere. Those stunning green eyes and the chestnut-colored hair set in a heart-shaped face were quite remarkable.

When she was within five feet of him, Maggie stopped in her tracks. Her eyes widened. "Finn? Is that you?"

Finn nodded. He smiled at her. All at once he felt like a little kid again. "One and the same," he drawled. "Hey, Maggie. It's nice to see you. Welcome back to Alaska."

He didn't know whether to hug her or shake her hand, so he did neither.

Maggie blinked and shook her head. "I can't believe it's you. I was expecting Declan."

"I work for O'Rourke Charters as one of the pilots," Finn explained. He didn't bother to mention he would soon be a co-owner of the company. Finn couldn't imagine her caring one way or the other. As a widow and single mother making a new life in Alaska, she had bigger fish to fry.

"You always did want to fly planes," Maggie said in a light voice. "Up to the wild blue yonder."

Hearing his grandfather's favorite expression tumble off Maggie's lips startled Finn. Killian O'Rourke had taught Finn and his younger brother Declan to fly. Finn's love of flying had come straight from his grandfather's heart. Killian had been a larger-than-life personality and the most loving man he'd ever known. The ache of yet another loss tugged at Finn. There wasn't a day in his life he didn't miss his grandfather and the man's steady influence and vast wisdom.

He inhaled a deep breath. Being back in Alaska after roaming around the country for several years meant having to deal with the past. So far, Finn wasn't sure he was doing such a good job of it. When he least expected it, old memories rose up to knock the breath right out of him. He shook the feelings off as he always did and focused on the here and now. Somehow he had to find a way to tell Maggie the specifics about his inheritance from Tobias. He prayed she wouldn't mind too much.

"Hi." The little voice startled him, serving as a reminder of Maggie's pint-size traveling companion.

"Hey. What's your name?" Finn asked, looking down at the small child standing beside Maggie.

Maggie tousled the boy's hair and said, "This is my son, Oliver. Oliver, this is Finn O'Rourke. A long time ago we were pals when I spent a few summers in Alaska with Uncle Tobias."

Finn stuck out his hand. Oliver looked up at his mother, then shook Finn's hand once Maggie nodded her approval. "Nice to meet you, Oliver."

"Are you our pilot?" Oliver asked, his expression full of wonder.

"Yep. I'm going to fly you and your mom to the best place to live in all of Alaska. There's moose and bears and fishing and reindeer pizza. Not to mention we have sled dogs and the northern lights."

Oliver's eyes grew big in his small face. "Whoa!"

"Are you excited about it?" Finn asked in a teasing voice.

Oliver nodded his head. "Mom says we're going to have our own house. We never had our own house before. And she's going to run a store." He rubbed his hands together. "And the best part is, she's going to find me a new father here in Alaska."

Finn felt his jaw drop. He swung his gaze toward Maggie. There was no doubt about it. Her expression showed utter mortification. He watched as she shot her son a look of annoyance. Oliver smiled up at her as if butter wouldn't melt in his mouth.

Finn reached out and grabbed Maggie's luggage and Oliver's bag. With a nod of his head he said, "Why don't we go board the seaplane and get ready for takeoff?" He winked at Oliver. "Love, Alaska, awaits you."

Once Maggie had settled Oliver into his seat on the seaplane, she sat down and buckled herself in. She couldn't remember ever having traveled in such a small plane before. She might have felt a little apprehensive if Finn O'Rourke hadn't been their pilot. Maggie knew instinctively they were in good hands. It was strange to feel that way since they hadn't been in each other's lives for quite some time, but Finn exuded an air of control and authority. And she knew he'd learned how to fly from the best—Killian O'Rourke.

As the plane took off, Maggie felt a burst of adrenaline race through her veins. They were really doing this! She and Oliver were on their way toward a brand-new life in the small hamlet of Love, Alaska. Maggie needed someone to pinch her. It was a surreal experience.

"Look, Mama. That mountain is ginormous!" Oliver's chubby, chocolate-stained finger pointed at a spot outside the window. She reached into her purse for a tissue, then wiped his fingers clean.

Maggie Richards chuckled at the excited tone of her son's voice as he pressed his face against the window of the seaplane. She leaned in and tousled his sandy head of hair, admiring his hazel eyes and infectious smile. No doubt she was biased, but Oliver was one adorable kid, even though he'd caused her a world of embarrassment with Finn at the airport. The look on Finn's face when Oliver had told him about getting a new father had been priceless. Finn hadn't known what to say and he'd looked at her with confusion etched on his too-handsome-for-his-own-good face.

Maggie hadn't bothered to explain her son's desire for a father in his life and her inability to convey to him that it wasn't something she could order on demand. Somehow Oliver had gotten it into his head that Maggie was going to find him a new father. Nothing she said or did could convince him otherwise even though the last thing Maggie wanted or needed was a husband. Been there. Done that.

Her heart ached a little bit as she observed her son.

He'd been through so much in his young life. If she had one wish, it would be to build a stable, peaceful life for him. Maggie was determined to create a strong foundation for Oliver in Alaska, and she would do it on her own as a single mother.

"Oliver, I'm not sure *ginormous* is an actual word in the dictionary."

Oliver turned toward her with confusion radiating from his eyes. He appeared crestfallen. "It's a word, Mommy. Honest."

She pressed a kiss against his cheek. "I believe you, sweetie." She reached for a napkin and wiped away the chocolate stains from the glass.

As she turned her head to peer out the window, Maggie let out a gasp as the majestic, snowcapped mountains came into view. Oliver was right. The mountains were ginormous. And magnificent. She couldn't remember ever seeing such a lovely vista in her entire life, even though she had traveled the world extensively before settling down to marriage and motherhood. How could she have forgotten this spectacular sight? Granted it had been twenty years ago, but some places deserved a lasting place in one's memory.

For most of the flight from the Anchorage airport, Maggie had been praying about this big move. Was she doing the right thing? By uprooting Oliver from their home in Boston she was taking him away from everything he'd ever known. On the other hand, she was determined to see her son grow up in a place where no one would judge him for his last name. Maggie had reverted back to her maiden name of Richards to avoid being blackballed. She had done the same for her son. He was now Oliver Richards. The town of Love wouldn't know their family history. They would be judged on their own merits and not based on news reports or local gossip.

Maggie let out a sigh. The last year had been devastating. Gut-wrenching. Her husband, Sam's death had left them reeling and trying to pick up the shattered pieces of their lives. Her beloved husband had been shot and killed while holding up a grocery store. In the aftermath, the bottom had truly fallen out of her world. Everything she'd thought about her life had been shattered in one devastating moment. To this day she still found it difficult to wrap her head around Sam's criminal actions or the fact that she'd been blind to them for so long.

But with this relocation to the other side of the country, a whole new world would be awaiting them. Uncle Tobias had bequeathed her his home in Love, as well as his shop, Keepsakes, and a nice sum of money. It would allow them to have a fresh start. That's what Maggie was calling it. She was relying on God to see them through the difficult weeks and months ahead. It wouldn't be easy to re-create a whole new life, but she knew it was important for Oliver's future and well-being.

Finn's voice buzzed in her ear through the headset.

"We're reaching our final descent. If you look out the window, you'll see beautiful Kachemak Bay stretched out as far as the eye can see. You might remember it from back in the day, Maggie. It's an Alaskan treasure."

Finn's voice was just as attractive as the man himself. It had been quite a shock for Maggie when she came face-to-face with her childhood buddy at the Anchorage airport. He was all grown-up now. With his dark brown hair and emerald-colored eyes, he was a serious looker. No wonder the town of Love had been luring women from all fifty states to their lovelorn town. If all the men looked like Finn O'Rourke, it was no small wonder Operation Love was such a successful campaign. Not that she wanted anything to do with it. Her dating days were over.

"It's awe inspiring," Maggie said into her mouthpiece. She turned and relayed the message to Oliver since he didn't have a headset on. "Pilot O'Rourke just reminded me of the name of the water down below. It's called Kachemak Bay."

Oliver wrinkled his nose. "Kacha what?" he asked. Maggie giggled at her son's attempts to pronounce the difficult word. Honestly, she could gaze at him all day long given the choice. This little boy was the joy of her life. She couldn't imagine how impossible it would have been to get through the past year without Oliver. Sam's death, and the circumstances surrounding it, had brought her to her knees. Her only saving grace had been Oliver. Sweet, funny Oliver.

"Kachemak Bay." She said the words slowly so Oliver could understand how to pronounce it. She listened as he repeated it several times in an attempt to get it right. "That's it," she said after the fourth try. "You said it perfectly."

"Yes! I did it." Oliver raised his fist in the air, his gesture full of triumph. A tight feeling spread across her chest. He seemed excited about their new journey. *Thank You, Lord. I've been so worried about him.*

Losing his father at five years old had been a catastrophic event for Oliver. She knew her son had a lot of emotions he'd bottled up inside him. And even though a year had passed, it wasn't a very long time for a child to grieve the loss of a parent. Oliver still struggled sometimes. He still asked for Sam. There were tears. And sadness. And tantrums. It broke Maggie's heart each and every time. Sam hadn't been a perfect father, but he had loved his son. And Oliver had been crazy about him.

Starting anew in Love, Alaska, might just be the very thing they both needed to get back on track and build a firm foundation for their future. They had been blessed by Uncle Tobias's generosity. The uncle she hadn't seen in twenty years had passed away four months ago. She had been remembered very generously in his will. Maggie felt a burst of joy at the realization that she was the owner of an establishment in a quaint Alaskan town. Between the shop and the house—it was so much more than she had ever dreamed of owning. Deep down inside, she didn't feel worthy of it all. But she would do her best to live up to Uncle Tobias's faith in her.

As the seaplane began to descend lower and lower toward the ground, Maggie gazed out the window and placed her arm around her son's shoulder. A shiver of excitement trickled through her. They were mere minutes away from landing in their new hometown. So much was riding on this brand-new adventure, particularly Oliver's happiness. Maggie hoped she'd made the right decision in bringing her child all the way to Love, Alaska.

* * *

Finn stood by the seaplane as Maggie and Oliver disembarked. He had grabbed their luggage and placed it on the pier for them. He looked around him at the familiar faces crowding around his two passengers. A small welcome committee had gathered to greet them at the pier, as was the custom when a newcomer arrived here in town. Finn smiled at the sight of the town mayor, Jasper Prescott, as he came toward them. With his long black coat and matching dark hat, Jasper cut a striking figure. Although he sported a gold cane, Finn knew it was purely an accessory. His wife, Hazel, walked by his side, her face lit up with a bright smile. Hazel and Jasper were newlyweds, having been married for less than a year. In many ways they were the heart and soul of Love.

Jasper reached out and wrapped Maggie up in a bearlike hug. "Howdy, Maggie."

He wasn't certain, but the look on Maggie's face seemed a bit overwhelmed by Jasper's enthusiasm. Or maybe Maggie was simply feeling the impact of this monumental move all the way across the country. He imagined having a kid added to the pressure.

This wasn't the first time a woman had come to Love with a child in tow. After all, Paige Reynolds had arrived a year and a half ago with sweet baby Emma in her arms—a big surprise no one had known about, including Emma's father, Cameron. It had all ended happily when Paige and Cameron walked down the aisle.

Maggie's son was a pretty cute kid, Finn reckoned. With his round face and hazel-colored eyes, he reminded Finn a little bit of himself at that age. He sure hoped Oliver's life was a lot more idyllic than his own had been. Although he had been a bit older when his mother passed away, the event had scarred him terribly and changed his life forever. Finn knew he'd never quite recovered from the trauma. Or the guilt.

Finn shook off the maudlin emotions. Things were looking up for him. He needed to be positive.

"Nice to see you again after all these years, Maggie," Hazel said in an enthusiastic tone. "Your uncle told us so much about you and Oliver over the years. He loved you very much." She reached out and enveloped Maggie in a tight bear hug.

Maggie's uncle Tobias had been a longtime resident of Love. He'd been an amiable man whose shop on Jarvis Street had always been popular. "Let her come up for air, Hazel," Jasper barked. Hazel let Maggie go, before turning toward her husband and scowling at him.

"Welcome back to Love," Jasper said in a booming voice. Maggie smiled at Jasper, which immediately lit up her face. With her delicate features, Maggie had a girl-next-door type of beauty.

Jasper turned his attention toward the little boy. "What's your name, son?" he asked in a robust voice. Finn let out a low chuckle at the look on Oliver's face. Much like everyone else who crossed paths with Jasper, Oliver seemed fascinated by his larger-than-life personality.

The boy looked up at Jasper with big eyes. "I'm Oliver."

Jasper stuck out his hand. "Hello there, Oliver. I'm

Jasper Prescott, the mayor of this town. Everyone calls me Jasper though."

"Hi, Jasper." Oliver stared, then frowned. "Hey! You kind of look like Santa Claus."

Finn knew that Jasper—with his white hair, blue eyes and whiskers—had heard this a time or two. The town mayor threw his head back and roared with laughter. "I like your honesty, young man." He winked at Oliver. "To tell you the truth, I sometimes feel like him. I do tend to spread a lot of cheer around this town." He winked at him. "Especially during this time of year."

Finn stifled an impulse to burst out laughing at Jasper's comment as Hazel rolled her eyes and let out an indelicate snort. Jasper frowned at his wife, then turned back toward Oliver.

"Would you like to head over to my grandson's café for some peppermint hot chocolate and s'mores?" Jasper asked, eyebrows twitching.

Oliver's hazel eyes twinkled. "S'mores are my favorite!" he said with a squeal of glee. He turned toward his mother. "Can we please go?"

Maggie reached out and tweaked her son's nose. "Of course we can. S'mores are my favorite too."

Finn watched the interaction between mother and son. Their tight bond was evident. He looked away for a moment, casting his gaze at the fishing boats docked by the pier. The boats served as a distraction from the feelings bubbling up inside him. A wave of longing for his own mother washed over him in unrelenting waves. He'd lived without her for almost twenty years, but the pain of her loss still lingered. It still gutted him when he allowed himself to think about it.

He didn't know why, but lately the memories had been coming at him fast and furiously. And the guilt he felt over her death never seemed to let up.

"Finn!" Hazel called out. "Would you like to join us?"

Finn turned his attention back toward the group. "I have a few things to do, but I'll meet you over there in a little bit. Don't worry about the luggage. I'll bring it over to the Moose."

"Thanks, Finn," Maggie said with a nod of her head. "We really appreciate it."

Finn didn't say a word in response. He merely nodded his head. Something about seeing Maggie again after all these years made him feel tongue-tied. She was so polished and put together. There was a regal air about her, although she didn't seem like a snob. She was miles away from the tomboy who'd run around with skinned knees and untied shoelaces. He doubted whether they would even have a single thing in common.

"We'll see you later then," Jasper said, clapping Finn on the back.

Hazel clapped her hands together. "Well then. What are we waiting for?" she asked, motioning for everyone to follow her down the pier. Finn watched as they all walked toward Jasper's car. At one point Oliver turned back toward him and waved. The thoughtful gesture made Finn smile. He waved back at him, getting a kick out of the way the boy's face lit up with happiness.

Finn was glad they were traveling by car. Even

though the Moose Café wasn't far, the ground was a bit slick from a recent snowfall. Maggie and Oliver weren't even wearing boots, he thought with a chuckle. Something told him it wouldn't take either of them long to figure out they were essential for Alaskan winters.

Once he was alone, his mind veered toward the pressing matter at hand—Tobias's bequest in his will. It couldn't have come at a better time. For weeks now he'd been in a financial bind. He'd needed to come up with a large amount of cash so he could buy into a partnership in O'Rourke Charters, his brother's business. So far his part-time job at the docks hadn't brought in much cash, and his hours spent working for O'Rourke Charters were few and far between. Living in a town recovering from a recession made finding a high-paying gig almost impossible. He was so close to achieving his dream of being his own boss. His financing had been approved, but for a lesser amount than he'd expected or needed.

Tobias had come to the rescue and left him a nice sum of money in his will. Although Tobias had placed a condition on receiving the funds, Finn couldn't be more thrilled about it. He clenched his jaw. Finn wasn't too sure how Maggie would feel about working side by side with him. Despite their past friendship, they hadn't been close in twenty years. The situation could prove to be very awkward. He no longer knew Maggie well enough to predict her reaction.

Just as the group departed in Jasper's car, another vehicle pulled up to the pier. It took only seconds for Finn to recognize it. He watched as his brother, Declan, got out and walked toward him. With his blond hair and movie-star good looks, Declan radiated charm. Until he'd married his wife, Annie, he'd been known around town as something of a ladies' man. Now he was enjoying the white picket fence and impending fatherhood. Although he was happy for Declan, Finn couldn't help but feel envious. That type of life wasn't meant for him.

"How'd it go?" Declan asked in an overly casual voice.

"Fine. Like always," Finn said in a curt voice. He didn't know why it bothered him so much to have Declan constantly checking on him. His brother must trust him since he employed him as one of his pilots. Yet, time and again, he gave Finn the feeling he was constantly peering over his shoulder. As the older brother, it didn't sit right with Finn. After all, for most of their young lives Declan had followed in his footsteps.

That was a long time ago, he reminded himself. Before he'd let Declan know he couldn't count on him.

Declan rocked back on his heels. "That's good," he said, quirking his mouth. Finn knew well enough by his brother's expression something was brewing. Declan was now shifting from one foot to another and clenching his teeth.

"What's going on? I know you didn't come down here just to say hello. Give it to me straight."

Declan quirked his mouth. "I need to firm up my plans regarding O'Rourke Charters. I know you said you were in, but I'm going to have to draw up contracts and take the final payment from you. Business has slid a bit even with the second plane, so I'd like to get moving on the purchase of a third one. I need for us to get moving on this partnership and secure more financing, as well as getting this infusion of cash from you."

Declan had been in a plane crash over a year ago. As a result, one of his planes—*Lucy*—had been damaged beyond repair. Because Declan had been trying to save money on his premiums on his insurance payments, he had reduced his coverage months before the crash. As a result, the policy hadn't fully covered the damages. Declan had managed to purchase a gently used seaplane a few months ago, but the company had taken a loss while operating with only one plane. Now his brother had his eye on a third plane in order to expand the business. Finn couldn't blame him for wanting to secure his company's future. Declan gave Finn flying hours as often as he could, but until he bought into O'Rourke Charters and they purchased another seaplane, Finn wouldn't be hired on as a salaried pilot. His dream of co-ownership would be on hold.

Finn scratched his jaw. "I know I've put you in a bind and I'm sorry about it."

Declan cut him off. "Finn, I'm not blaming you for not getting all the financing you needed, but I've been as patient as I can for the last few months. The bottom line is I've got to make some serious decisions about the future of O'Rourke Charters. If you want to join forces, I'm going to need us to sign a contract and have you make a substantial contribution to buy your way into the business."

"Declan, I'll be honest with you. I wasn't sure how I was going to come up with the last portion, but my prayers have been answered." Finn reached into his jacket pocket and pulled out the paperwork he'd received yesterday afternoon.

"What's this?" Declan asked as Finn handed him the documents.

"I got a visit yesterday from Lee Jamison. He's the executor for Tobias's will." He shook his head, still in disbelief over his windfall. "Believe it or not, Tobias left me a nice-sized sum of money."

Declan raised a brow. His eyes scanned the paperwork. He let out a low whistle as he swung his gaze up to meet Finn's. "Tobias was mighty generous. You know what this means right? There are conditions."

Finn nodded. "Yes. I'll have to help Maggie get the shop ready for its grand opening, then help her get it up and running for a total period of no less than four weeks. At such time the shop successfully opens, then I'll get my inheritance." Finn repeated the terminology he'd memorized from the paperwork. "Then I can buy my way into O'Rourke Charters."

Declan let out a hearty chuckle. He slapped Finn on the back. "I can't believe it!" He grinned at Finn. "You always do land on your feet."

"Not always," Finn said, "but thanks to Tobias, we're going to be partners."

More than anything, Finn wanted to be a co-owner of O'Rourke Charters. He wanted it more than he'd desired anything in his life. For so long he had denied how great it felt to be up in the wild blue yonder flying a plane. But he couldn't stuff it down any longer. It was where he was meant to be and being a pilot was his destiny. From the very first time his grandfather had taken him up in the air and let him fly the plane, Finn had been a goner. Killian had told him it was his destiny. Being co-owner of O'Rourke Charters would give him stability and respectability. It would give him a purpose. It would allow him the opportunity to live out a lifelong dream. And even though his grandfather wasn't around any longer, perhaps he could still make him proud.

"Four weeks will be fine," Declan said with a nod. "I can work with that."

Finn grinned at his brother. It felt as if a huge weight had been lifted off his shoulders. "I appreciate it. And I'm not going to let you down this time. I promise."

"You better not," Declan said, his blue eyes flashing a warning. Finn knew he was referencing the countless times Finn had bailed on him in the past. Not this time, he vowed. He was no longer the man he used to be. Finn liked to believe he'd grown and matured over the past few years. He wasn't walking away from things anymore. Finn was done with running away from home and everything he held dear.

Declan turned back toward him. "I'm really happy for you, Finn. And for our future partnership. I really do want this to work out."

"Me too," Finn murmured as Declan turned away and continued back down the pier. Once his brother was out of earshot, Finn murmured, "Things are going to work out. They have to."

Now all he had to do was explain his inheritance from Tobias to Maggie and break it to her about the stipulation requiring him to work side by side with her at Keepsakes. Finn let out a deep breath. He wasn't sure what he would do if she objected. Would he still be eligible for his inheritance if she declined his help? His whole future now hung in the balance.

Chapter Two

Maggie found herself smiling as they pulled up in front of the Moose Café. As they'd driven down Jarvis Street, with its old-fashioned charm and festive holiday decorations, the quaint downtown area of Love had captivated her. Although she'd visited on three occasions as a child, her favorite had been during Christmastime. She'd been overjoyed to experience the town decked out in all its holiday glory. Those same feelings were rising up within her at this very moment. Nostalgia warmed her insides.

A fully decorated Christmas tree sat on the town green while pine wreaths and red ribbons graced every lamppost lining the street corners. This town was getting ready for the holiday, even though it was a month away.

She'd been a little surprised to see Uncle Tobias's shop all shuttered up as they drove by. It stood out amid all the other festively decorated shops. Keepsakes looked abandoned and neglected. Maggie didn't bother to point it out to Oliver. She didn't want him to be disappointed so soon after their arrival.

Poor Uncle Tobias, she thought. He had loved his shop so much. How she wished things hadn't been so tumultuous in her own life for such a long time. Perhaps she could have relocated to Love a year ago and helped out her uncle. Once Maggie entered the Moose Café alongside Jasper, Hazel and Oliver, the tinkling sound of the bell above the doorway welcomed her. As soon as she crossed the threshold, she noticed sprigs of holly dangling down from the ceiling. The interior of the establishment was decked out in Christmas decorations. Wreaths. A fully trimmed Christmas tree sitting in a corner. She noticed all of the waitstaff were wearing T-shirts with moose on them. Delectable odors assaulted her senses. Her stomach began to grumble, serving as a reminder that they hadn't eaten in several hours. And she wasn't sure the quick snack of pretzels and fruit they'd grabbed at the Anchorage airport even counted.

Oliver—her finicky eater—often needed to be encouraged to eat more. As it was, he practically lived on pizza, french fries and chicken nuggets. She looked down at him, eager to know his feelings at every point in their journey.

"This place is cool!" Oliver said, his voice brimming with enthusiasm. Maggie felt herself heave a little sigh of relief. It was so very important that Oliver embrace their new hometown. Maggie didn't think things would work out in Love if her son wasn't happy. After all he'd been through, Oliver deserved to be joyful.

And so do I, she reminded herself. Oliver wasn't

the only one who had been put through the wringer. As a mother it was easy to ignore her own needs, but she vowed to do better at being a more content, well-rounded person.

Maggie followed the trail of her son's gaze. He was looking at a pair of antlers hanging on the wall. He couldn't seem to take his eyes off them. Although the vibe of the Moose Café was rustic and a bit on the masculine side, Maggie could see a few feminine touches. Red-and-white carnations sat on each table. Soft, romantic paintings hung on the walls. It gave the establishment a nice, eclectic atmosphere.

"Thanks for the thumbs-up." A deep male voice heralded the appearance of a chocolate-haired, green-eyed man. He greeted them with a warm smile and patted Oliver on the back. "Those antlers are pretty awesome, aren't they?"

Oliver bobbed his head up and down in agreement. He flashed the man a gap-toothed smile.

"Cameron!" Jasper called out, addressing the dark-haired man. "We need a table for four, please." He gestured toward Maggie and Oliver. "This is Tobias's niece, Maggie Richards. You two might have met back when Maggie visited Love as a child." Jasper flashed her another pearly smile. "Maggie, this is my grandson, Cameron Prescott. He owns this delightful establishment." Pride rang out in Jasper's voice.

Cameron stuck out his hand by way of greeting. "Nice to see you again after all these years. It's been a long time. I'm happy to hear you'll be opening up Keepsakes soon."

"It's wonderful to be back," Maggie said. "And I'm very excited about the shop. Oliver and I have been very blessed by Uncle Tobias." Maggie didn't even have the words to express her gratitude about this opportunity. Her heart was filled almost to overflowing.

Maggie had vowed to be more courageous in her life. Fear had always been such a stumbling block. It was one of the reasons she'd stayed with Sam for so long and put up with his run-ins with the law and his inability to hold a job.

If anyone had told her a year ago that she would move to Alaska in order to run her uncle's shop, Maggie never would have believed them.

"And we're very grateful to have you back in Love," Hazel added. It had been Hazel who had called Maggie to tell her about her uncle's death. Then weeks later she'd called again to direct her to call the executor of her uncle's estate to inquire about her inheritance.

Upon hearing all the details about her inheritance, Maggie wanted to pinch herself. In one fell swoop, her entire life had changed. She grinned at Hazel. Maggie couldn't believe she was standing next to the impressive woman who had created the genuine Alaskan Lovely boots that had taken the country by storm. Uncle Tobias had told her all about Hazel's creation of the boots and the way the town of Love had set up a business to mass-produce them.

Maggie couldn't really put her gratitude into words without explaining about the major losses she'd endured and the shameful circumstances of Sam's death. It had cost her everything she'd worked so hard to build for her family. And she couldn't afford to talk about it to anyone in this town. She'd uprooted her entire life in order to start over here in Love. And she wasn't going to tarnish it by revealing her deepest, darkest shame.

Maggie wanted to be respected in this town. She wanted her son to be free of any stigma.

Maggie felt a tug on her sleeve. "Mommy. Can I go over to the jukebox?" She looked down at Oliver, who was pointing toward a tomato-red jukebox sitting in the corner of the room.

"Why don't I show you how it works?" Cameron suggested. "Make yourselves comfortable at any table you like."

Cameron walked away with Oliver at his side. Maggie watched them for a moment, feeling wistful about the lack of men in her son's life. It made her ache to remember how many nights Oliver had cried himself to sleep over his father.

"Tobias told us about the loss of your husband when it happened. He was heartbroken for you and Oliver." Jasper turned toward her and cleared his throat. "Maggie, Pastor Jack told us about the tragic circumstances."

Maggie felt her eyes widening. A wild thumping began in her chest. The jig was up. Her secret had been exposed. "How did he know about it?"

"He contacted the pastor at your church to find out if we could do anything to make your transition to Love any easier. Although we already knew you were a widow, we didn't know the specifics."

"W-what did Pastor Baxter tell him?" she asked, her heart in her throat. *Lord, please don't let everyone here*

*in Love know already about Sam holding up the gro-
cery store. I want to protect my son. He's innocent in
all of this. It will be just like back home all over again.
Name-calling. Finger-pointing. Judgment.*

Jasper looked at her with sad eyes. "He told Pastor
Jack that your husband was killed in a grocery store
holdup." He made a tutting sound. "It's so very tragic
for your family." He began patting her on the back.

Maggie felt her shoulders slump in relief. She felt
horrible for allowing this version of the story to go un-
challenged, but for Oliver's sake she had to keep quiet.
He'd endured enough. And he was just a little boy. She
couldn't let the sins of the father be visited on the son.

"Grief is a process, Maggie. We know you're probably still trying to wrap your head around such a pro-
found loss." Jasper's blue eyes became misty. "Never
fear. We're here for you. We're going to make sure y'all
have a joyful holiday season."

"Thank you, Jasper. I feel very blessed to receive
such a warm welcome here in Love." Maggie blinked
several times, doing her best to hold back the tide of
tears.

Suddenly, Oliver came racing to her side. "Mom.
Sophie said I can go in the kitchen and make my own
pizza."

Sophie—the beautiful, Titian-haired waitress standing behind Oliver—was smiling down at her son as if
he'd hung the moon. This town really was full of genuinely kind folks.

"Oliver is going to help me make a masterpiece,"
Sophie said with a grin. The Southern twang and the

red-and-white Santa hat perched on her head only made her appear more adorable, Maggie realized.

"That sounds like fun," Jasper said with a nod. "I think I'm going to come with you and take some notes so I can whip up a pizza at home."

Hazel let out a groan. "That's all I need," she groused. "I can already smell the burned pizza."

Jasper scowled at Hazel.

"Come on, Jasper," Oliver said, tugging at the mayor's sleeve.

The look etched on Oliver's face said it all. There hadn't been a lot of smiles or laughter in the last year. Lately, Oliver had begun to turn a corner, but his grief had been all consuming for such a long period of time. He had shrunken down into a quieter, less joyful version of himself. Maggie wanted the old Oliver back, the one who laughed with abandon and didn't seem afraid of the world around him. With Christmas coming in four weeks, she wanted Oliver to experience the wonder of an Alaskan Christmas.

At least for the moment her son seemed to be over the moon. She prayed this new adventure didn't get old. Love, Alaska, was a small, quaint town where everyone knew each other. Maybe over time they would be embraced by the townsfolk.

Once Oliver headed toward the kitchen with Jasper and Sophie, Hazel turned toward Maggie. Compassion flared in her eyes.

"There's no need to fret, Maggie. I'm the only one here in town who knows the truth about the holdup. And I'm not about to share your personal business with anyone, not even my husband," Hazel said in a reassuring tone. "It's not my story to tell."

Maggie looked over her shoulder to make sure no one might overhear her conversation. "Thank you, Hazel. I appreciate you keeping it in confidence. I really don't want everyone to know Sam was killed while holding up the store," Maggie said in a soft voice. "I just want a clean slate."

Hazel reached out and patted her on the shoulder. "Everyone deserves a shot at getting their life back on track. God loves you, Maggie. And pretty soon, this whole town will consider you and Oliver as one of our own."

One of our own. Just the idea of it caused tears to pool in Maggie's eyes. It was the very thing she hoped to establish for her son here in Love. She let out a sigh. Hazel knew her shameful secret, but thankfully she wasn't going to divulge it to anyone.

Rather than being an innocent victim, her husband, Sam, had been the gunman holding up the grocery store. And he'd been shot in the process, losing his life and making their son fatherless. The ensuing media attention had been a vicious whirlwind. Maggie had been the recipient of hate mail, harassing phone calls and even a few death threats. She had been fired from her job and they had lost their housing.

This opportunity for a fresh start was a blessing from God. And Uncle Tobias. He had loved Maggie so much he'd laid out all the groundwork for her to rebuild her life in his hometown.

Most people wouldn't believe it, but Maggie had been

totally clueless about Sam's illegal activities. In the end, she had paid dearly for believing in her husband. For loving him so much she'd had blinders on.

"Never again," she murmured to herself as Hazel led her toward a table. In her humble opinion, love led to hurt and pain, loss and disillusionment. She had no interest in going down that road again. She was going to focus on her son and his well-being. She would be both mother and father for Oliver. Maggie wouldn't be looking for love in this small fishing village.

Romance could go knock on someone else's door.

Chapter Three

By the time Finn made his way to the Moose Café, his stomach was grumbling like a grizzly bear. Even though he was short on money these days, his belly hadn't gotten the message.

Finn tried to stuff down the feelings of frustration with himself. In many ways it felt as if the past year had been about starting over from scratch. Although he had made positive strides, he was still miles away from where he wanted to be in his life. He couldn't help but envy Declan.

While he'd been backpacking his way around the country and avoiding any hint of responsibility, Declan had been building up his company and cementing his ties here in Love. Now his younger brother was a newlywed and soon-to-be father. For a man like himself, who had always rejected the notion of settling down, Declan's life looked pretty idyllic.

You're not cut out for all that, he reminded himself. *It would all just fall apart, just like everything else.*

Finn smiled at the reindeer-and-candy-cane wreath gracing the door of Cameron's establishment. He knew his friend had a zany sense of humor. Everyone in town had gone holiday crazy right after Thanksgiving, even though Christmas was still a few weeks away. He sauntered into the Moose Café, eager to grab a bite to eat. Although his stomach urged him to order a big meal, he knew his budget wouldn't allow it. Every extra nickel he had would go into his savings account.

The moment he entered Cameron's establishment, a warm feeling came over him. Even though the food was stellar, Finn knew he frequented the Moose Café for the cozy, down-home atmosphere. It was a feeling he'd been seeking his entire life but hadn't yet found on a personal level. A place to call home.

The sound of hearty laughter drew his attention to a table dead center in the dining area. His eyes went straight toward Maggie. She was laughing and he could see the graceful slope of her neck as she reared her head back.

Maggie was one of the most attractive women Finn had ever encountered. He felt a stab of discomfort as he realized she might soon be joining the ranks of Operation Love. After all, most women who arrived in the small fishing village came to town in the pursuit of a romantic match.

It didn't take a rocket scientist to figure out that men would line up in droves for an opportunity to date the beautiful single mother. Beauty was in the eye of the beholder, but in Finn's humble estimation, Maggie

Richards was the most stunning woman who had ever stepped foot in Love, Alaska.

He shrugged off thoughts of Maggie. She was way out of his league and he needed to keep his eye on the prize and not get distracted by thoughts of sweet-faced, green-eyed women. It had been a long time since he'd been romantically involved with anyone. Way too long according to Declan.

So far Finn himself had rejected the idea of being paired up with anyone. Although he didn't disapprove of Jasper's matchmaking program, Finn had learned a long time ago that he wasn't the home-and-hearth type. His fractured childhood was proof enough for him.

"Hey, Finn!" Hazel called out to him, waving him over toward her table. "Come over and join us."

Finn walked over to the table, greeting Sophie along the way as she gracefully carried a tray full of food and drinks. "I'll be right over to take your order, Finn," Sophie said with a nod.

"Just bring me a bowl of the soup of the day and a coffee," Finn said.

The only available seat at the table was right next to Maggie. Finn tried not to stare at her as he sat down. It was a near-impossible task. The light scent of her perfume rose to his nostrils. It smelled like vanilla and roses. He couldn't think of the last time a woman had sparked such a response in him. For so long now he'd just been going through the motions and avoiding getting close to anyone. Even his family.

Maggie leaned a bit toward him. Her voice flowed over him like a warm breeze. "I forgot my manners earlier, Finn. Thank you for getting us safely to Love on your seaplane. You're an amazing pilot."

He locked gazes with her, marveling at the deep green color of her eyes. "You're quite welcome. It was my pleasure. I think it's safe to say flying is in my DNA."

She grinned at him, showcasing dimples on either side of her mouth. "Your parents must be very proud, as well as your grandfather. Back when we were kids he really fawned over you and Declan. Killian thought the two of you had hung the moon."

Finn felt his face fall. Maggie had no idea about his mother's death or the circumstances surrounding it. He felt a little ache at the prospect of dredging up painful memories. There was no point in dodging it. Sooner or later, someone would tell Maggie about it and she would wonder why he hadn't mentioned it.

"My mother passed away quite a while ago. Actually, it was shortly after the last time you visited Love." He looked down at the table and began fiddling with his fingers. He might as well tell her everything. "My father left Love years ago. He pretty much fell apart after my mother died. And my grandfather passed on when we were in our late teens."

She let out a sharp gasp. "Oh, Finn. I'm so sorry to hear that. You've lost a lot over the years."

The sympathetic tone of her voice made him cringe. He didn't want to be the object of anyone's pity, especially not Maggie's.

"I had no idea," she continued. "My mother and Uncle Tobias had a falling-out not long after we left

Alaska, so for many years there was an estrangement. I only got back in touch with him a few years ago. We were able to pick up right where we left off."

"He mentioned something about the falling-out. Tobias was really thrilled when you reached out to him. Your uncle and I became good friends over the years."

Maggie twisted her mouth. "I wish that I could have made it back to Love a long time ago." She let out a little sigh. "I'll always regret it."

"Tobias always dreamed of you coming back," Finn acknowledged, "but he understood you had your own life to live in Boston."

Oliver walked up to the table and stood close by his mother's chair.

Maggie nudged him in the side. "Sweetie, don't you have something to say to Mr. O'Rourke?" She shook her head. "I mean, Finn."

Oliver slowly moved closer to Finn. For a second it seemed as if he was having trouble looking Finn in the eye. When he did look up, his hazel eyes were full of wonder.

"Thanks for bringing us here." He chewed his lip for a moment. "I think one day I wanna be a pilot just like you."

"That's fantastic, buddy," Finn said, reaching out and tousling Oliver's hair. "One of these days I can take you up in one of the planes if your mom says it's all right. I can show you the local area."

Oliver's mouth hung open. Everyone at the table laughed. The sound of Maggie's tinkling laughter warmed Finn's insides. Much like the woman herself, it was charming.

"Can I go, Mom? Can I?" The pleading tone of Oliver's voice was endearing.

"It sounds like a fun excursion," Maggie conceded. "I think we can make it happen." Maggie sent Finn a grateful smile. Oliver let out a celebratory hoot as if he'd won a battle. His enthusiasm made Finn feel ten feet tall. He wasn't used to being viewed as important. That's how the kid made him feel. It was a nice change from thinking of himself as useless.

He stared blankly at the menu, trying to shake off the desire to look over in Maggie's direction. There was no sense in him denying it. He felt a pull in her direction. And what man wouldn't? he asked himself. She seemed like the whole package. Looks. Brains. And he knew from their past she had a lot of heart. But Finn had determined a long time ago he wasn't suited for romance. And it was clear from where he was sitting that a woman like Maggie was the sort you brought home to Sunday dinner with the folks. She wasn't one to be trifled with.

Just then Sophie appeared at the table with a tray of food. Thankfully it gave Finn something to focus on other than the woman seated to his right. She placed a bowl of soup down in front of him, along with a hearty-looking sandwich with kale chips on the side. Finn shot her a look of gratitude. Sophie winked at him. As his friend, she knew his financial situation was dodgy. This was her way of helping him out.

Finn took a huge bite of his sandwich, then sampled

the lobster bisque, one of Cameron's specialties. He flashed Sophie a thumbs-up sign.

Instead of heading back to the kitchen, Sophie stood at the table with a concerned look etched on her pretty features.

"What's wrong, Sophie?" Jasper asked. "You look like you burned something in the kitchen," he teased.

Sophie's eyes darted over to Maggie. She bit her lip. "Agnes Muller just called. She knows it's Jasper's tradition to bring folks over to the Moose to welcome them to town, so she figured you might be here. She said she's been trying to reach Maggie since this morning."

Maggie looked down at her phone and let out a sound of frustration. "Oh, I had my ringer off. She's going to be Oliver's babysitter when he starts kindergarten in a few days. It'll only be for a few hours in the afternoon since he'll be in school till the early afternoon, but since I want to get the store up and running quickly, she'll be a big help." Maggie stood up. "Let me go call her back in case it's something important."

Finn's gaze trailed after Maggie as she walked over to a private area of the café to make her phone call. Even from a distance of twenty feet, Finn could tell something was wrong. Maggie's face crumpled. The look of distress stamped on her face was evident.

He looked away, reminding himself it was none of his business. The last thing he wanted to do was get wrapped up in somebody else's problems. The good Lord knew he had enough of his own to focus on.

"Did something happen to Agnes?" Hazel asked Sophie. Her brows were furrowed, eyes full of worry.

"She didn't say too much but she's at Liam's clinic," Sophie answered, referencing Dr. Liam Prescott, Jasper's grandson and brother to Cameron, Boone and Honor. "She wanted to talk to Maggie first, but she sounded pretty weak, if you ask me."

Hazel made a tutting sound. "Lots of folks have been coming down with the flu. I pray she rebounds quickly if that's what's ailing her."

All eyes were on Maggie as she returned to the table. It was evident something had happened to turn her sunny mood into a somber one.

"Is everything all right?" Finn asked, the question hurtling off his lips.

Maggie pushed her hair away from her face with a trembling hand. "Agnes took a bad fall this morning. She sprained her ankle and she's on crutches. There's no way she's going to be able to watch Oliver now while I'm working, which puts me in a real bind." Maggie threw her hands in the air. "I don't know what I'm going to do."

Maggie's stomach was tangled up in knots as she provided the explanation about Agnes's ankle. She felt a little numb. Her mind was whirling to try to come up with a plan B. Although she felt terribly for Agnes, she now had to worry about getting a replacement for the woman she'd hired as a sitter. Oliver was a great kid, but at his young age it would be hard to keep him entertained while she worked nonstop to get Keepsakes in tip-top shape. In order to capitalize on the Christmas season, Maggie needed to open up the shop as soon as possible. And after seeing the worn sign outside the shop, Maggie had the feeling her work was cut out for her.

The ramifications of the situation roared through her with a mighty force. Finding Agnes had been no easy task. This was a small town with few options for part-time childcare.

She sank back down into her seat and stared mindlessly at the table. She didn't want to panic about the situation, but she had no idea what she was going to do. Maggie needed the income from Keepsakes. Although Uncle Tobias had left her money in his will, she knew the importance of establishing a nest egg. She planned to stash most of the money in a bank account and live off her proceeds from the store.

Maggie glanced over at Oliver. Thankfully he was in his own world, munching on his pizza and seemingly oblivious to the unfolding drama. He was so sensitive these days. She didn't want him to worry about who would be taking care of him while she was at work.

"We'll just have to find somebody to fill in for Agnes," Hazel said. Maggie had the feeling Hazel was trying to sound chipper for her benefit.

"That might be easier said than done," Jasper responded with a frown. "Why don't you write down the particulars? Hours and salary. Anything you feel is pertinent to the position. I'll circulate it around town hall and see if anybody bites."

Maggie let out the breath she'd been holding. The mayor of Love was making it clear she wasn't alone in this. Gratitude rose up inside her. She'd felt so terribly isolated and alone for the last year. It was nice to know things in this town might be quite different for her and Oliver.

Maggie ferreted around inside her purse and pulled out a small notebook and a pen. When she was done writing, she ripped the page out and placed it down on the table before sliding it toward Jasper.

He looked up at Maggie and twitched his eyebrows. "Not many hours since it's an after-school position, but I'll post it up. You might get a teenager looking for hours like this."

A teenager! How in the world could she leave her son with someone so young? Maggie knew it wasn't out of the ordinary, but in her world it was. Being over-protective of her son was a by-product of having her husband taken away from her in such a tragic way.

"I appreciate anything you can do. Problem is, I need to hire someone as soon as possible. I need to get this resolved so I can get the shop up and running." Maggie felt her voice becoming clogged with emotion. Everything had been working so smoothly until this rug had been pulled out from under her.

Anxiety grabbed ahold of her. Despite her desire to be courageous, she found herself faltering. For most of her life, Maggie had struggled with anxiety. It tended to rear its ugly head in times such as this one when she felt things were spiraling out of her control. Other times it just struck her out of the blue. She took slow breaths to steady herself, reminding herself that she wasn't dying or in danger, even though it felt like it when anxiety overwhelmed her.

"I think you need to get some rest, Maggie. You've been traveling all day and pretty soon jet lag is going to settle in." The rich timbre of Finn's voice startled her. For the most part he'd been sitting at the table as a quiet observer. His green eyes were sure and steady as they locked with her own. "I think a good night's rest will help you."

Maggie nodded, knowing his words were true. She wanted to check out their new house and unpack some of their things and take a hot shower before crashing. Oliver needed a bath and a good night's sleep. "That's a good idea," she said, feeling grateful to Finn for sensing she was at her limit. She looked over at Oliver. His eyes were beginning to droop. She felt a twinge of guilt for not noticing how tired her son looked.

"I'd like to get going. Oliver is about to conk out. I'd appreciate a ride over to the house," Maggie said.

Jasper jumped to his feet. He bowed in Maggie's direction. "Jasper Prescott at your service. Get your coats on and I'll drive you over there."

Finn stood up from the table. "Why don't I drive them home, Jasper? I already have their luggage in my car," Finn suggested. "It's in the same direction as my house."

"Perfect!" Hazel said in a boisterous voice.

"Thanks, Finn," Jasper said, slapping Finn on the back. "There's a booster seat by the doorway. We picked it up the other day for Oliver based on Maggie's instructions."

"I'll grab it on my way out," Finn said.

"Let me just run to the kitchen," Hazel announced.

"I've got a few pans of food I cooked for you and Oliver, Maggie. I hope you like lasagna, salmon and tuna casserole. You'll also find a few things at the house. Staples like pasta, cereal, milk and bread." She beamed at her. "This way you won't have to worry about grocery shopping or meals for a few days."

"That's really sweet of you, Hazel," Maggie said, feeling grateful for such generosity. She couldn't think of a single person in Massachusetts who would have gone out of their way for them. Despite the worry about finding a replacement for Agnes, Maggie had the feeling God had planted her and Oliver right where they needed to be.

Her son stood up and put his jacket on. Maggie reached down and zipped up his down coat. December in Alaska was frigid. Although Boston got cold, it couldn't compare to this type of biting weather. She reached into her purse and pulled out her son's hat. Before she could place it on Oliver, he'd moved away from her.

Maggie watched as he raced over to Finn. "What kind of car do you have?" Oliver asked, his face lit up with excitement. Her son seemed to have a sudden burst of energy. No doubt it was due to Finn.

Finn chuckled. "I drive an old truck. It's pretty cool though since it belonged to my grandfather. I fixed it up and got it back in running condition. Guess what color it is?"

Oliver scrunched up his face. "Um…baby blue like a robin's egg?"

"Nope. Not even close. It's as red as Santa Claus's suit."

"Whoa," Oliver exclaimed. "That must be awesome."

Something told Maggie that Oliver was developing a pretty strong case of hero worship. He seemed to think everything about Finn was cool. Finn had sealed the deal by offering to take Oliver up in one of his planes. She felt a twinge of envy. Maggie couldn't think of the last time Oliver thought she was the bee's knees.

"I'm going to go outside and warm up the car so it's not freezing inside. I'll meet you guys out front in a few minutes," Finn said. He held up his palm and Oliver high-fived him.

Maggie knew she should feel grateful for Finn's offer to drive them to their new house rather than worrying about Oliver's reaction to him. After all, Finn had already done his job by flying them to Love from Anchorage. She shivered as she watched her son's gaze trailing after Finn. A fatherless boy would look for father figures anywhere and everywhere. She didn't want Oliver to get any ideas about her childhood pal being his new daddy.

Finn. He'd sure grown up into an extremely good-looking man. She imagined he drew lots of interest from the females in town. Not that she was looking! Maggie had no interest in romance, which was ironic considering she was smack in the center of Operation Love territory. She was well aware of the program since she'd read the newspaper articles and seen the television shows highlighting Mayor Jasper Prescott's matchmaking campaign.

Love, Alaska, was Maggie's shot at redemption. God had blessed her by making her a mother. She owed

Oliver a stable, loving home. It was her responsibility. Although her childhood buddy seemed like a nice guy, Maggie had no intention of getting fooled again by good looks and a smile. Romance wasn't on her agenda.

Love had certainly made a fool of her in the past. It had cost Maggie so very much. Her peace of mind. Dignity. Her reputation. Sam had betrayed her and Oliver. Now, she was solely focused on her son and creating a safe, emotionally healthy world for him. His needs came first. Oliver might want a father, but Maggie definitely didn't want a husband. She was determined to raise her son by herself and be both mother and father to him.

Maggie needed to keep her eyes on the prize. She had to focus on getting the shop ready for the grand opening and find a sitter for Oliver for the hours he wasn't in school. A whole new world was opening up for them. Maggie wasn't going to squander these opportunities.

Chapter Four

As he walked toward his truck Finn let the frigid blast of wintry air wash over him. He'd come outside so he could warm up the car for Maggie and Oliver and place the booster seat inside his truck, but it also provided him with him a few minutes by himself so he could reel in his thoughts.

Although the situation with Agnes was terrible for Maggie, he couldn't stop thinking about the timing. Tobias's will stipulated that he needed to help Maggie set up Keepsakes and provide assistance with the grand opening. Perhaps part of helping Maggie could be watching Oliver after school let out so he wouldn't be underfoot while she set up shop. He could be the part-time sitter.

Finn wasn't a childcare expert by any means, but he had ties to the community, a way with kids and a fun-loving personality. And for the next few weeks he could devote himself to the position, until such time as he could collect his inheritance from Tobias. While

Oliver was in school he could help Maggie with setting up the store and ordering any inventory she needed, as well as doing any heavy lifting. By the time four weeks elapsed, Agnes could very well be on the mend.

It would be win-win for everyone.

The truck had considerably warmed up by the time Finn spotted Maggie and Oliver standing in the doorway of the Moose Café. Maggie held a large shopping bag in her hands. He imagined it contained the meals Hazel had prepared for the two of them. Finn stepped down from the driver's seat and walked Oliver and Maggie across the street to his truck. He helped Oliver step up into the cab, then took the bag from Maggie before lending her his hand, which felt so small in his larger one.

Once she was buckled in, Finn closed the door and made his way over to the driver's seat. As Finn began to drive down Jarvis Street, he found himself pointing out local places of interest. He could hear pride ringing out in his own voice.

"The sheriff's office is right across from the Moose Café," Finn said, gesturing toward the building. It had been festively decorated with wreaths and red ribbons.

"Is there really a sheriff who works there?" Oliver asked in an awestruck tone.

Finn nodded. "Of course there is. His name is Boone Prescott. He's Cameron's brother. And he happens to be a friend of mine in case you'd like to meet him."

"Whoa. I've never met a real-life sheriff before," Oliver said in a gushing tone. "I've only seen them in movies. I hope when I meet him he shows me his shiny gold badge."

Finn chuckled, enjoying seeing things through Oliver's fresh eyes. Love was a wonderful town, full of heart and connections and fortitude. The townsfolk had pluck and grit. For many years he hadn't appreciated his hometown. He'd been too busy trying to stuff down the painful aspects of his childhood. Running away and avoiding all the memories had been the easier path.

And in the process he'd also placed a wedge between himself and Declan. He wanted them to be close again, and they were slowly getting there.

"Oh, what a charming bookstore," Maggie said, turning to gaze out of the window at the Bookworm shop. "The holiday decorations really make the store come to life."

Finn nodded in agreement as he took a quick glance at the whimsical window display. Maisie had really gone overboard this year. Sugarplum fairies and dancing reindeer with glowing noses, as well as chubby snowmen and falling snowflakes. He wasn't usually sappy about Christmas, but there was something about the decorations that brought out his sentimental side. Finn couldn't help but think back on the wonderful holidays he'd spent with his family before the bottom had fallen out of their world.

His parents had always gone the extra mile to make sure they knew the true meaning of Christmas. The emphasis on the birth of Christ had been at the forefront, but there had always been surprises waiting for them under the Christmas tree—train sets and skateboards and dirt bikes. One year his father had gifted his mother with a toy poodle she'd named Pippin. Finn smiled at the memory of his mother squealing with joy.

"There's Keepsakes," Finn said, slowing down as they passed the boarded-up shop. It would have been odd if he hadn't pointed it out. Truthfully, the shop had seen better days. Numerous townsfolk had deliberated over whether to fix up the exterior before Maggie arrived in town. In the end, it had been the general consensus that since Maggie was now the legal owner, only she could make the decision as to how Keepsakes should look.

He watched as a myriad of emotions crossed Maggie's face. Finn reached out and patted her hand. "Don't worry. All it needs is some spit and polish. You'll get it done in no time at all."

Although Maggie nodded in agreement, the look emanating from her eyes was full of trepidation. He wished there was something more he could say to make her feel confident about her new venture.

Finn continued to point out landmarks—the post office, the trading post, the newly opened hair salon, the toy store and the pawnshop. Finn slowed down as they approached the library.

"Right there is the Free Library of Love. My sister-in-law, Annie, works there as head librarian." He glanced over at Maggie. "They have a great children's section."

"It's beautiful," Maggie said. "I can't wait to explore this town at my leisure. There have been a lot of changes since I was last here."

"As you may remember, it's a small town," Finn conceded. "But it's full of treasures. I think you'll be very content here once you settle in."

Finn continued down the snow-covered streets, taking a left as he turned off toward the mountain road. It was bit more difficult to navigate than the main streets in town. Finn had learned to drive on these roads so he knew it wasn't anything he couldn't handle. But he worried about Maggie living out here and driving into town. He made a mental note to remind her about taking safety precautions and outfitting her vehicle properly with all-wheel drive and studded tires. Although she hadn't mentioned it, he assumed Maggie had also inherited Tobias's truck.

The sound of Oliver's chatter filled the silence once Finn ran out of things to say. He didn't know how to explain it, but there was something about Maggie that made him feel tongue-tied. That fact would probably make his brother laugh out loud since as a kid he'd always complained about Finn never shutting up.

Once he spotted the mailbox announcing they had reached Twelve Mountain Court, Finn turned down the long driveway and drove past tall snowcapped pine and spruce trees until he reached the house. The log cabin was a modest size. Perfect for a small family. In Maggie and Oliver's case it would be more than enough. He parked the car right in front, then jumped out of the car to grab the baggage.

"Can I help?" Oliver's little voice sounded just behind him.

He turned around and handed Oliver the smallest piece of luggage he could find. "Thanks for helping out." Finn walked behind Oliver. The corners of his mouth twitched as he watched the child using all his strength to carry the bag. This kid sure had pluck.

Maggie led the way to the front door, pulling out a set of keys and opening up the house for them. As they stepped over the threshold, the smell of cinnamon floated in the air. Finn placed their belongings down by the staircase.

On the hallway side table sat a bowl of pinecones emanating a wonderful scent. A big fruit basket sat next to it. A bowl full of candy canes sat nearby. Maggie walked over and reached for the card placed on the table. She began to read it out loud. "'Enjoy your new home. Blessings! Your new friends in Love.'" A small sound escaped her lips. To Finn's ears it sounded a little bit like a sob. Maggie wasn't facing him, but he could see her wiping at her eyes.

"Mommy, why are you crying?" Oliver asked. "I don't like to see you cry."

"Maggie, are you all right?" Finn asked as a strange tightening sensation spread across his chest. The thought of Maggie awash in tears deeply bothered him.

She turned around to face them, sniffing back tears. "I'm fine. I'm just a bit overwhelmed at their generosity. Everyone in Love has been so kind to us, including you, Finn." Gratitude shimmered in her eyes. "I'm very thankful."

"You're quite welcome," Finn said. "It's one of the things I love best about this town. The people here sure do know how to roll out the red carpet. I'm just glad those are happy tears."

Oliver looked up at Finn. "She cried a lot when my dad died."

An awkward silence settled over them. Finn didn't know how to respond to Oliver's innocent statement. Clearly, Maggie didn't either.

He knew from personal experience how devastating it felt to lose a parent at such a tender age. His heart ached for Oliver...and Maggie.

"Oliver, why don't you head upstairs and check out your new bedroom?" Maggie suggested, steering the conversation away from the uncomfortable topic. Oliver took off and began racing up the stairs, the sound of his footsteps echoing in the silence.

"You two must be exhausted." Finn could see the slight shadows under Maggie's eyes. He needed to get out of her hair so she could explore her new digs and enjoy some downtime. A sigh slipped past Maggie's lips. "This day has been truly a blessing, but I am tired. It's a long way from Massachusetts to Alaska."

There wasn't any point in dragging his feet any longer. He'd been waiting for a moment alone with Maggie so he could broach the subject of Tobias's will. He needed to tell her about the stipulation whereby he would be assisting her with her new store.

"Maggie, I need to tell you something."

The serious tone of his voice caused a wrinkle to appear on her forehead.

"Okay. What is it?" she asked, her voice sounding tense.

"Tobias left me a sum of money in his will," he explained.

Maggie's features relaxed. She gifted him with a sweet smile. "That's wonderful, Finn. He was always crazy about you back when we were kids."

"Tobias believed in me. He made me feel I could do anything I put my mind to if I tried hard enough. Over the years he became an honorary grandfather to me." He shifted from one foot to another, then shoved his hands in his front pants pockets. "He loved you very much, Maggie. He talked about you all the time. I think that must be why he put a special stipulation in the will. In order to get the inheritance, I need to help you get the store up and running. Specifically, for a period no less than four weeks."

Maggie let out a surprised sound. She knit her brows together. "What? Why would Uncle Tobias have placed such a condition on his bequest?"

Finn ran his hand over his face. "I think he was worried about it being too much for you. He knew you'd been through a lot, having lost your husband last year and being a single mother. I believe he thought he would be making things better for you by giving you someone to help out with everything." Finn let out a ragged sigh. "And I know he was trying to help me. It's pretty humbling. Frankly, this couldn't have materialized at a better time for me. He knew that I needed an infusion of cash to buy into my brother's aviation business."

"That was Uncle Tobias's way, wasn't it? Even as a kid I remember all the times he tried to help Mama." She twisted her mouth. "She went from relationship to relationship, marriage to marriage—dragging me with her all across the country. Bless him. Uncle Tobias tried his best to turn things around for us, but it didn't work."

"He was a good man. And an even better friend." Finn missed Tobias more than mere words could convey. There hadn't been many people in his life who'd believed in him without reservation. It was because of his encouragement that Finn had approached Declan about becoming a partner in O'Rourke Charters. And now, thanks to Tobias's generosity, his long-held dream was within reach.

"I appreciate all of Uncle Tobias's efforts on our behalf," Maggie said. "To be perfectly honest, I'm going to need all the help I can get so Keepsakes can open as soon as possible." She made a tutting sound. "Leave it to Uncle Tobias to realize I couldn't do it all on my own."

"He believed in you. I know that for a fact," Finn said. "He said it all the time."

"Thanks for saying so. I don't ever want to let him down," Maggie said. "I want to do everything in my power to make Keepsakes successful."

"And I know you're looking for someone to watch your son while you're getting the shop up and running."

Maggie nodded. "Yes, I am. Do you happen to know of someone? I'm racing against the clock to find a reliable caregiver."

"I understand," Finn said, stroking his chin. "It's hard to focus on Keepsakes with an energetic six-year-old running around."

"If you know of anyone reliable to watch Oliver I'd be very grateful. As you can see, he's a sweet boy. A little high-spirited, but a good kid."

Finn cleared his throat. He shifted from one foot to the other. "Well, actually, I do know of someone."

Maggie's face lit up like sunshine. "You do? That's wonderful. Who is it? Maybe I can interview them tomorrow."

He gazed directly into Maggie's eyes, hoping she would see his sincerity. "It's me, Maggie. I could help watch Oliver."

Maggie wasn't certain she'd heard Finn correctly. "Did you say that you want the job? As Oliver's babysitter?"

"Yes," he said with a nod. "Not permanently or anything. I just figured since I'm already going to be helping you out at Keepsakes I could watch Oliver after he gets off from school. That way you would still be able to take care of business at the store and I would still technically be fulfilling the conditions of the will. I'd still be helping you with the store during the hours before Oliver gets out of school."

Maggie's head was spinning. Finn had thrown her a curveball. Although she knew Finn, so many years had passed by since they had truly known one another.

"What experience do you have with watching children?" she asked, wondering how she could let him down easy without hurting his feelings. She had never imagined hiring a man to watch her son. Finn didn't strike her as a babysitter.

"Not a lot really," Finn confessed. "But I used to be a head counselor at an overnight camp and I watch Cameron's daughter, Emma, from time to time. I'm honest and fun loving." Finn grinned. "Kids really like me. Just ask Hazel or Jasper. They can vouch for me."

She tugged at her shirt. "Well, that's all fine and good, but I need a qualified professional to watch my son while I'm working."

"*Need* being the operative word, Maggie. You're in a bind. Truthfully, so am I. I need to fulfill the terms of Tobias's will so I can partner up with my brother. That means we have to get Keepsakes in tip-top shape so it can open up as soon as is humanly possible. Working with your son underfoot could be problematic. This could be a mutually beneficial situation."

Maggie locked gazes with Finn. "I appreciate your offer, but I don't think it would work out."

He narrowed his gaze. "And why is that, Maggie? When you think about it, it's perfect. You've known me since we were kids. I'm not the bogeyman. Oliver already knows me. And he likes me. I'm trustworthy. You and your son's lives were in my hands when I flew you here from Anchorage. Surely you can see that?"

Suddenly, Maggie felt annoyed at Finn for putting her on the spot like this. "It isn't about liking or not liking someone. Yes, that's important, but I need to find someone who's a good fit overall."

"I know you probably think a woman's touch is best, but you're wrong. Oliver could benefit from spending time with a man. It's written all over him."

Maggie bristled. Who did Finn think he was to tell her what her son needed? "Oliver is fine," she said in a crisp voice. "I give him lots of love. He isn't lacking anything. His father passed away quite suddenly a year ago. It's been hard wading our way through the shock and grief, but I've been acting as both mother and father for him. I've been doing the best I can."

Finn held up his hands. "It wasn't meant as an insult. I just know—I know what it's like to lose a parent at a young age." His voice softened. "I know what he's going through firsthand. It's a long process."

"I know," she said in a clipped tone. "I've been walking with him every step of the way." She hated the defensive tone of her voice, but it felt like Finn was telling her she wasn't doing a good job with Oliver. It hit her in her most vulnerable place—her fear of not being a decent mother to her son.

"You know what? Forget I said anything," Finn said. "I apologize for upsetting you. I just thought we both could make lemonade out of lemons. Forgive me. I shouldn't have brought it up."

He quickly moved toward the door, turning back to her from the threshold. "Good night, Maggie. If you want to hit the ground running with the store, I can meet you there first thing tomorrow morning. With four weeks until Christmas, we're really pressed for time. Ideally, if you can get the shop open in two weeks you can still rake in some great proceeds from holiday sales."

Maggie let out a squeak. "Two weeks?"

Finn nodded. "Keepsakes has always been a big holiday-themed shop on Jarvis Street. It's a Christmas staple here in town. The shop was shuttered last year a few months after the holidays. At the time no one knew Tobias was sick, so it perplexed a lot of folks."

She chewed on her lip. "I don't want to lose out on

holiday sales, especially if people are anticipating it being open this year in time for Christmas. Why don't we meet at Keepsakes at nine? That way I can let Oliver sleep in and then get him breakfast before I head to town."

"Do you need me to swing by and pick you guys up?" Finn offered.

"Thanks for the offer, but Hazel gave me the key to Uncle Tobias's truck. I'll make sure to take it easy down the mountain road." Part of Maggie wanted Finn to come pick her up, but she knew it was important to start doing things for herself. She didn't want to take the easy way out. The thought of driving down the mountain road was a bit scary, but she was determined to face it head-on.

"Well then, I'll meet you in front of Keepsakes tomorrow morning. And welcome to Love." He opened the door and disappeared into the frosty Alaskan night.

"'Night," Maggie called out after him. She shut the door behind Finn and leaned against it. She felt completely exhausted after her long journey, the news about Agnes and her awkward discussion with Finn about Oliver. She let out a ragged breath.

"Why don't you want Finn to watch me?" She turned toward the sound of her son's voice. He was sitting at the bottom of the steps staring at her with big eyes.

"Oliver, what have I told you about eavesdropping on adult conversations?"

"I wasn't. At least not on purpose." There was a sheepish expression etched on Oliver's face. "I was thirsty, so I came back downstairs."

Maggie walked over to the staircase and reached for her son's hand. "Let's go get some water."

Once they were in the kitchen, Maggie went over to the cupboard and pulled out a mug. She turned the faucet on and filled it halfway. Oliver sat down at the kitchen table and Maggie handed him the water.

"Why don't you like Finn?" he asked before taking a generous sip of water.

Maggie gasped. "I do like Finn. We were friends when we were kids. And he's a really great pilot. But that doesn't mean I want him to be—"

"My manny?" Oliver asked.

Maggie couldn't help but giggle. "Manny? Where in the world did you hear that expression, Oliver?"

"Back home one of the kids in my class had one. *Manny* is a male nanny," he explained in a matter-of-fact tone.

"I know, Oliver. But I had no idea you would know."

"I know a lot of things. More than you think I know." Oliver's sad expression tugged at her heartstrings. Maggie wasn't sure she wanted to know what Oliver was talking about. Did he know more about Sam's death than she'd ever realized? She prayed it wasn't true. It was such a horrible thing for a little boy to wrap his head around.

"You're getting to be such a big boy," Maggie said, wishing she could turn back time to when Oliver was a little toddler in diapers. He was growing by leaps and bounds.

"I like Finn. A lot. It would be super cool if he could watch me while you're setting up our new store." Oliver was now pleading with her.

"It makes sense that you like him. But I need to

have faith in the person who watches you. That doesn't come easily."

"He flew us all the way here in his seaplane. You trusted him to do that."

Sometimes Oliver's maturity shocked Maggie. He was wise beyond his years. There was nothing she could say to refute his statement. It was the truth.

"I appreciate your opinion, but this is something Mommy has to decide on her own. It's grown folks' business," Maggie said in a gentle voice.

Oliver rolled his eyes and groaned. "I hate when you say that."

Maggie chuckled at the look etched on her son's face. A feeling of immense love for Oliver hummed inside her heart.

As Maggie prepared for bed a little while later, thoughts of Finn's proposition continued to float through her mind. Was it really so out of the question? What had she really known about Agnes before she'd offered her the position? Surely she knew way more about Finn. After all, they'd been childhood playmates. More than that, she realized. They'd been besties.

Best friends forever. Hadn't they promised each other they would always be friends? And even though two decades had passed, she still felt as if she knew Finn. He seemed different, but deep down she sensed he was still the same comical, lovable boy. Would it be such a grand leap of faith to trust him to care for Oliver?

Oliver's pleas ran through her mind as she began to drift off to a peaceful sleep. Had she made a huge mistake in dismissing Finn's offer to watch Oliver?

Chapter Five

Bright and early the next morning, Maggie woke up to greet the first day of her new life in Alaska. While Oliver was eating a bowl of cereal, she went out on the back porch and took in the breathtaking vista stretched out before her. White-capped mountains loomed in the distance. Although the December air was frigid, it was clean and crisp. She let out a gasp as she spotted a majestic eagle soaring in the air. She couldn't look away from the bird's graceful moves. It made her feel centered and peaceful.

She shoved her hands in the pockets of her heavy winter coat. It was pretty cold out here, but she felt helpless to tear her gaze away from the view staring back at her. In all her life she had never seen such pristine land.

"I did it," she said in a triumphant voice. Despite all of her fears, Maggie had gathered up her courage and traveled all the way to this quaint fishing village. She was transforming her life. And she was now officially a business owner. Keepsakes might need some sprucing up, but from her childhood recollections, it had been a wonderful shop specializing in heartwarming treasures. It had always enjoyed a loyal, solid clientele.

She was going to be working side by side with Finn thanks to Uncle Tobias's directive in his will. Leave it to her uncle to protect her even after his passing. Maggie didn't have any friends in Love, and even though her friendship with Finn went back decades, she still felt connected to him. And she needed his friendship. He had always been a source of light and laughter. Maggie could sorely use it now as a newcomer to a town where everyone seemed to know each other. She and Oliver were basically strangers here in Love, despite their connection to Uncle Tobias.

The past year had been filled with an aching loneliness Maggie couldn't even put into words. Finding acceptance here in Love would be life altering. As she stood and stared out across her two acres of land, Maggie felt incredibly blessed. The past had been nightmarish, but the future felt hopeful.

Thank You, Lord. For blessings great and small. Even though I've doubted Your presence in the past, I know You must be here with me. I've felt You. At times it seemed like a push against my back, propelling me forward when I didn't even think I could get out of bed. At other times I felt this groundswell of confidence building up inside me.

A sudden rapping sound rang out behind her. When she turned around, Oliver had smashed his face against the glass patio window and was making funny faces at her. Maggie grinned at her son's goofiness. There was no question about it. Oliver seemed less stressed and happier since they had arrived in Alaska. Maybe there was something in the air here.

A half hour later, Maggie began the drive to town from her new home. According to Hazel, Uncle Tobias's truck had recently been serviced by an auto body shop. Maggie appreciated the gesture. Having reliable transportation was of vital importance. The roads were packed with snow and there were a few slick spots. Maggie drove very gingerly. Thankfully, she was proficient at driving in wintry conditions due to the years she'd lived in New England. She just needed to focus on that aspect instead of giving in to her nerves about Alaskan road conditions.

Oliver sat in his booster seat, pointing and gesturing toward anything of interest he spotted outside his window. The toy store was of particular interest to him.

"Mom! Look at that toboggan! I'm putting it on my Christmas list," he shouted, his voice brimming with enthusiasm. "I could really fly on it."

Maggie smiled and made a mental note to purchase the toboggan for Oliver. He deserved something spectacular.

She would make sure this Christmas was full of surprises and blessings and dreams come true for Oliver. A toboggan would be really special for his first Christmas in Alaska. Years ago Maggie and Finn had flown down the mountain at Deer Run Lake on matching sleds. Finn had surprised her by writing her name in indelible ink on one of the sleds. Maggie chuckled at the memory of how angry Declan had been about Finn giving his sled to Maggie.

Thankfully, her phone's GPS had guided her perfectly to Uncle Tobias's shop. *My shop*, she corrected herself. It was hard to wrap her head around her new reality. In one fell swoop Maggie was a home owner, as well as the owner of a business and a truck. Her life had never been filled with so much promise.

Thank You, Lord, for all of these blessings.

Maggie felt startled by all of the spontaneous prayers she'd been uttering since arriving in Alaska. It was the second one today.

It had been a very long time since she had spoken on such a regular basis to God. They had come to a crossroads back when her life fell apart and Sam died in such a shocking manner. Maggie shivered as the memories of that terrible time crashed over her in unrelenting waves. It had felt as if the entire world had turned against her. Except for Uncle Tobias. He had soothed and comforted her, even though unbeknownst to her, he was dealing with his own terminal kidney issues and dialysis at the time. Her chest tightened as she remembered his invitation to come live with him in Alaska.

"Maggie, my door is always open for you and Oliver. Just say the word and I'll buy the plane tickets for you."

"That's very generous of you, Uncle Tobias. I'm wary of uprooting Oliver so soon after Sam's passing. But it's nice to know I have options," she'd told him.

"You'll always have a home here in Love," he'd told her in a voice clogged with emotion.

He had continued to invite her until his health condition had deteriorated. By the time Maggie discovered Uncle Tobias was so ill, he'd been in his last weeks of life. Maggie wasn't sure she would ever forgive herself for not being by Uncle Tobias's side in the last moments of his life. Why hadn't he told her about his illness? She had the feeling he hadn't wanted her to go through another ordeal after what Sam had put them through. Maggie still wished she'd known Uncle Tobias was so sick. It would have added an urgency to his invitation. For all intents and purposes, he had been her closest family member with the exception of Oliver. She couldn't even count her mother, since their relationship was estranged.

A soft tapping on her window drew her out of her thoughts. Finn was standing there with a determined look on his face. In the clear light of day, she wasn't sure how to feel about him helping her put the shop in order. Although they had once been the best of friends, they were now essentially strangers. *Doing it all by myself would have felt empowering.* She prayed Finn wasn't going to try to boss her around or take control of things. Maggie had put up with a lot of that behavior in her marriage to Sam. She wouldn't stand for it again!

She let out a sigh. She needed to stay positive and stop blocking her blessings. Even though decades stood between them, she knew Finn was a good person. Perhaps working side by side would help them get back to a place in time where they'd been able to finish each other's sentences. It would be nice to get her best friend back. And if Finn overstepped with regards to the shop, she wouldn't hesitate to tell him to take a step back.

"Finn!" Oliver cried out, unbuckling himself and practically vaulting out of the car.

Maggie stepped down from the driver's seat, watching as her son threw himself against Finn. She winced at the sight of it, filled with worry about Oliver getting so attached so soon. It wasn't her son's way to be so demonstrative.

"Oliver! Give Finn some breathing room," Maggie said, gently pulling Oliver away.

"It's okay. No one ever gets this excited to see me except my dog, Boomer," Finn said with an easy grin.

Oliver looked up at Finn. "You have a dog? What kind?"

"He's a rescue. Part terrier and part Labrador. My friend Ruby Prescott pointed him in my direction. She trains search-and-rescue dogs."

"Do you think she could find one for us?" Oliver asked.

"Slow down, cowboy," Maggie said with a chuckle. "A dog is a big responsibility. We need to settle in first before we make such a big decision about a pet."

Oliver stuck his lip out and sent her a mournful look.

Finn, clearly seeking to distract Oliver, clapped his hands together. "Why don't we go check out the shop?" he asked. "I'm sure Uncle Tobias has plenty of things inside to capture your attention. Maps. Puzzles. Maybe even a periscope."

Oliver nodded enthusiastically, seemingly forgetting he was disgruntled with his mother. Maggie sent Finn a look of gratitude.

They began walking toward the storefront. Maggie stopped in her tracks and looked up at the shabby exterior. The windows were completely covered with heavy brown paper, making it impossible to see inside.

The sign was weathered and worn, clearly in need of a fresh coat of paint. A long-ago memory tugged at her. A beautiful sign in a cherry-red color. It was a simple fix, she realized. One she could take care of herself with a fresh can of red paint and a ladder. She would make sure it was restored to its former glory. Thankfully, Hazel had made arrangements on her behalf to have the electricity turned on in the shop.

She turned toward Finn. "How long has the place been closed?" Maggie asked.

Finn shrugged. "About seven months, give or take. It was open last Christmas per usual. Tobias started feeling poorly and then lost the desire to keep the shop open. For a long time though no one knew he was ill. He kept it close to the vest."

A feeling of guilt swept over Maggie. If she had accepted Uncle Tobias's invitation to move to Alaska a year ago, perhaps she could have kept the store open and helped take care of her uncle. At the time she hadn't been ready to make such a major life change. It was a missed opportunity, one she would regret for the rest of her life.

Maggie took the keys out of her purse and dangled them in the air. "Here we go." She inserted the gold key in the lock. As soon as she turned the knob and pushed the door open, a musty scent filled Maggie's nostrils. The interior was dark. All she could see were shapes and stacks of things piled up. She let out a cough as dust tickled her nostrils.

"Let me turn the lights on." Finn's arm reached out and he fumbled along the wall for a few seconds before the lights came on. The shop was now flooded with light. Maggie let out a shocked gasp. The entire shop was one big mess. Not a single surface was clear. Boxes had been strewed everywhere. Some were even piled up on top of each other.

"Oh my word," she said, raising a hand to her throat. Maggie blinked, hoping it was an optical illusion rather than reality staring her in the face.

The entire place was in disarray. As her gaze swung around the establishment, Maggie was finding it difficult to even make sense of the layout. She spotted a counter and a cash register but there were random items piled up along the space.

"What in the world?" Finn exclaimed. He was standing behind her with Oliver at his side. How she wished her son wasn't here to witness this.

"This place is a wreck!" Oliver said, walking past Maggie and peering around him.

Maggie reached for her son's arm to stop him from venturing around the store. Things were stacked up high. It was very possible something could fall on top of him and he could get hurt.

"No one's been in here since Tobias shut up the shop," Finn said. "I had no idea this place looked like this. It's probably why he shuttered up the windows." Finn had a stunned expression etched on his face.

Maggie shook her head. She felt sick to her stomach. "I—I don't know what to think. This place isn't even close to being ready for a grand opening." Tears pooled in her eyes. Once again, she felt as if the rug had been pulled out from under her. She hadn't expected the place to be in pristine, ready-to-go condition, but nothing had prepared Maggie for the ramshackle appearance of the store.

"I think Mommy is going to cry again," Oliver said to Finn in a loud whisper.

Finn met her gaze. She tried her best to blink away the tears. She felt a few tears slide down her face. It was embarrassing. Maggie wanted to be a courageous person. Not someone who broke down every time she came upon a roadblock.

"I'm not crying, Oliver," she said in a shaky voice. "I've just got a little dust in my eyes."

"It is dusty in here," Oliver said, scrunching up his face as if he smelled something rotten.

Suddenly, she felt Finn's arm around her shoulder. He pulled her close to his side and began patting her on her shoulder. It felt comforting and solid. It had been such a long time since she'd been held up by a man's strong arms. For the first time since she'd come back it seemed as if no time at all had passed since they'd been inseparable running buddies. Finn had always been good at drying her tears over skinned knees and squabbles with her mother.

"It's going to be all right, Mags," he said, using his childhood nickname for her. "All this means is that we have our work cut out for us. We can do this."

Her lips trembled. "B-but Christmas is only a month away. It's important that I hit the ground running so I can take advantage of holiday sales."

Finn nodded. "I agree. Those holiday sales are crucial, which means we've got to get this place in tip-top shape. Starting today."

She sniffled. "You're right. I'm just afraid it will all fall apart," she confessed. "I knew everything seemed too perfect."

"Be strong and courageous. Do not be afraid or terrified because of them. For the Lord, your God, goes with you; He will never leave you nor forsake you," flowed from Finn's lips.

Maggie was familiar with the Bible verse, but it had been quite some time since she had cracked open a Bible. His words were comforting. They settled around her like a warm, cozy blanket.

"I know this must seem overwhelming," Finn said, "and I totally get it. You weren't expecting to see the place look like this."

She shook her head, her hair swinging around her shoulders. "I thought maybe there'd be a little dust and a few cobwebs. A few boxes stashed in the corner." She threw her arms wide. "But this! It seems a bit like a hoarder's dream."

"It's not as bad as all that." Finn looked around the shop. "This place needs some TLC. You're probably an expert at that, right? You're a mom. You've changed dirty diapers and wiped messy chins and faces. Mothers are warriors. Just think of this as taking care of a child, one who is totally dependent on you."

Maggie chuckled. Taking care of a child was nothing like clearing up this tornado. But at least she could find humor in it. Finn had made her laugh at a moment when she felt deflated. Just like the old days. When they'd been ten years old Finn had brought humor and light to her life. The two summers and one Christmas she'd spent in Love palling around with Finn had been the best days of her life. He'd always had the ability to make her laugh. After all of these years, he still did.

She took a steadying breath. Finn was right. This place needed some serious TLC. Uncle Tobias had gifted her with a magnificent inheritance. He had made it possible for her to change her circumstances. She'd had to fight her whole life just to keep her head above water. And even though she was terrified, Maggie wasn't going to give up without a battle.

She placed her purse down on a nearby counter after wiping it down with a towel, pushing aside a few boxes in the process. She unzipped her down jacket and tossed it on a chair covered with plastic. She turned back toward Finn and Oliver then dramatically pushed up her sleeves.

"Let's get to work, boys. We need to get this place set up for the Christmas rush."

Finn let out a roar of approval. He raised his arm in the air in a triumphant gesture. Oliver, looking like a pint-size version of Finn, did the exact same thing. Maggie didn't have time to worry about Oliver's instant bond with Finn. Who wouldn't be crazy about the man? He was charming and funny and he had the cutest smile she'd ever seen.

Maggie looked away from the distracting sight of Finn O'Rourke. She had a job to do. She was laying the foundation for a solid future in this town. If they could get Keepsakes ready to open in two weeks, it would be the best Christmas present of all.

* * *

After a few hours of trying to make a clear path through the mess and organize some of the merchandise, Finn realized Oliver was fading fast. The kid was practically bouncing off the walls and desperate to leave the store. Every few minutes Maggie would have to stop what she was doing to see to Oliver's needs. At this rate, Finn figured, it would be Easter before the place was cleaned up.

It wasn't a fair situation for the kid, Finn reckoned. He was too little to help and too young to understand why he couldn't. Something needed to be done so they could focus without interruption on the shop. Finn's entire future was riding on the successful reopening of Keepsakes.

Finn excused himself for a few minutes, then placed a call to Ruby Prescott, his dear friend and wife to his childhood buddy Liam Prescott.

"Hey, Ruby. It's Finn. I need a huge favor."

"Name it," Ruby said.

Finn wasn't surprised by Ruby's quick response. She was easygoing and sweet by nature. Beloved by the whole town. Adored by her husband, Dr. Liam Prescott, and their son, Aidan.

"I was wondering if Aidan is available for a last-minute playdate. To make a long story short, I'm helping out Tobias Richard's niece, Maggie. She arrived in Love yesterday and we're down at Keepsakes trying to get it up and running. Her son, Oliver, is with us. He's right around Aidan's age. So I figured—"

The sound of Ruby's tinkling laughter came across the line. "Poor thing. I'm guessing he's bored silly."

"That's putting it mildly. And to be honest, this place is a bit of a wreck," Finn admitted. "He really shouldn't be here until we get things more organized."

"I guess that explains why the windows were shuttered. Poor Tobias was such a proud man. He probably just became overwhelmed." Ruby made a tutting sound. "Why don't we drive down and meet you over at the Moose Café? Oliver can have lunch with us and then I'll bring him back to our house so the two boys can hang out together. You can swing by and pick him up later this afternoon. How does that sound?"

Finn exhaled. "Sounds like you're a lifesaver."

Once he hung up with Ruby, Finn pulled Maggie aside to tell her about his phone call. The moment he saw Maggie's expression, Finn worried that he'd made the wrong move. Maggie didn't seem so thrilled with his having set up a playdate for Oliver.

"I'm just not sure I'm comfortable leaving Oliver with someone I don't know."

"Well, Ruby's a good friend of mine. I trust her implicitly. And you and I are old friends, Maggie. You can trust my judgment."

Maggie bit her lip. Finn could see the concern swirling in her eyes.

He reached out for Maggie's hand. He squeezed it tightly. "Trust me. I wouldn't put Oliver in a dangerous situation."

"I get anxious about my son, Finn. He's all I have," Maggie said in a low voice. She turned and looked at

Oliver, who was sitting down and playing with an electronic device.

"It may sound silly to you, but when we lost his father so suddenly it made me really fearful of something happening to Oliver. All at once, life seemed really fragile. I guess you could say I lost my courage." She made a face. "I suppose it's safe to say I haven't gotten it back yet."

Finn nodded. His throat felt clogged with emotion. "I know what it's like to lose someone you love very suddenly. It throws you completely off balance. It makes you question everything. I think you need to remind yourself of how far you've come." He winked at her. "After all, you made a huge move to Alaska and you're about to open up your own shop. That's not for the faint of heart."

"I don't want Oliver to pick up on my fears." She cast another glance at her son. "He can go on the playdate. He needs to be a little boy. And making a new friend his own age will be good for him."

Finn grinned at Maggie. "He'll love Aidan. And Ruby's the best. Now you and I can start unpacking some of these boxes without worrying about something toppling down and hurting Oliver."

"Sounds like a party," she said in a teasing voice.

Finn smiled at her joke. He felt relieved she was loosening up a little bit. Although he could tell she was a fantastic mother, Finn sensed she was a little bit tightly wound. The fact that she had agreed to the playdate was a good sign. He admired her for having the pluck and grit to drastically alter her life by moving to Alaska.

After what she'd been through, he knew it couldn't have been easy. The past had the power to get in the way of a person's future.

Even after all these years, Finn still struggled with his own past. Just when he thought he had moved beyond it, the memories rose up to cast a shadow over the present. He prayed Maggie would find a way to find closure and embrace her new life.

Not only for herself, but for Oliver as well.

Leaving Oliver with Ruby and Aidan wasn't easy for Maggie. But meeting Ruby Prescott had left Maggie with a warm feeling about the woman. With her dark hair and café au lait–colored skin, Ruby was a radiant beauty. She seemed down-to-earth and kind. And like Maggie, she was a mother to a young boy. Aidan seemed like an amiable, content little charmer. Oliver and Aidan had quickly warmed to one another. When she left the Moose Café in order to head back to the shop, the trio was ordering lunch and the boys were giggling over a shared joke. She didn't know whether to laugh or cry over the fact that Oliver didn't even seem to notice her departure.

Small steps, she reminded herself. Everything in Alaska was new to her and she needed to accept the fact that her little boy was growing up. He would always be her baby, but she needed to allow him to spread his wings.

"There's stuff in here that needs to be tossed," Finn noted. He was standing with his arms folded across his chest. He looked handsome and authoritative. Maggie felt thankful he had been here with her when she had first opened up the shop. It had been an absolute shock to see Keepsakes in such a shambles. Back when she'd been a kid, the store had been in pristine condition. Having Finn at her side had made it bearable. It was a comfort to know she wasn't alone in this. She still harbored childhood memories of helping Uncle Tobias stock shelves and playing with the cash register. Sweet, enduring memories etched on her heartstrings.

"Why don't we make a toss pile and a viable-merchandise pile?" Maggie suggested.

Finn wiped his arm across his brow. "Sounds like a plan. You also should start coming up with prices. Once everything gets settled you can look online and research how much the items are worth to make sure you're on track." He held up a silver frame. "Some of them still have tags on them."

Maggie nodded.

They began working in companionable silence. She could hear Finn rustling around by the back of the store. She was tackling an area by the front counter. So far she hadn't come across any of the Christmas items. She needed to get her hands on them so she could come up with a festive window display and set up the front of the store with seasonal items.

She looked over at the front window and envisioned creating a beautiful Christmas display to attract customers. Perhaps a lovely nativity scene or something with lots of bells and whistles.

After an hour of searching through boxes, Maggie finally hit pay dirt.

"Whoa. I think I just stumbled upon the Christmas merchandise." She lifted the lid off one box and began to poke around inside it. There was an abundance of items. Individually packaged ornaments. Tiny Christmas village display items. Christmas flags. Festive banners. Light-up lawn displays.

Maybe she could set up the Christmas village in the window. It would look beautiful with all the little houses lit up and blanketed with fake snow.

Finn wiped his brow with the back of his hand. "That's great. All of that stuff needs to be front and center as soon as the shop opens."

Maggie tugged at another box. It was sitting off to the side with nothing placed on top of it. When she opened the lid she saw mounds of tissue paper. She reached in and gently began unveiling the items. She let out a cry of delight as she laid eyes on the delicate snow globe. Inside was a snowman and a little girl. She shook it a little and watched as snowflakes began to swirl around inside. Maggie let out a sigh. She'd always wanted a snow globe collection. Her mother had considered her request as too extravagant for a child, so her wish for one always fell on deaf ears. After all these years, she still loved the beauty and grace of the glass creations.

"Snow globes. This whole box is filled with them." She held one up for Finn to see. "Isn't this exquisite?"

"Nice," Finn said with a nod of approval. "Those will fly off the shelves."

Maggie ran her fingers over the smooth surface of the snow globe. It was so beautiful she almost wished she could keep it. But she couldn't get sentimental over the items. The whole point in owning a shop was to sell merchandise for a profit.

You're not a kid anymore, she reminded herself. It was silly to feel sad over a snow globe she had never received for Christmas.

"Are you a snow globe enthusiast? You can't take your eyes off that one," Finn said.

"I guess so," Maggie said with a nod of her head. "I've never owned one, although as a kid I found them fascinating."

"You seem to feel the same way as an adult," Finn teased.

"I suppose I've always been drawn to them." Maggie gently placed the snow globe back in its box. She imagined a customer would pay a good amount for it.

"So tell me about Operation Love," she called out to Finn, hoping to distract herself from bittersweet memories. "I read a little about it on the internet, but you've seen it up close and personal—the successes, the failures." Maggie had been invited to sign up for the program weeks ago, but it wasn't something she was considering. For someone who had been burned by love, joining the town mayor's matchmaking initiative would not be a prudent idea. Finding love was not her objective in Alaska, although she was still curious about the program.

"It's been great for this town. For so long there was a female shortage. The male-female ratio was really unbalanced. It still is, but it's not as bad. And there are lots of couples who've gotten engaged and walked down the aisle as a result. Do you remember Boone Prescott? Declan's best friend?"

Boone! Dark hair, intense eyes and a quiet disposition. Boone had been joined at the hip with Finn's brother, Declan. He'd been the type of kid who had sat back and watched everything around him. It didn't surprise her how he'd ended up in law enforcement.

"Boone met his wife, Grace, through the program." Finn chuckled. "Grace came here as a participant in Operation Love, although she was really working undercover as a journalist to write a story about the program and the townsfolk. They had a few bumps along the way, but they found their happily-ever-after."

"What about you? Have you signed up?" she asked, imagining Finn would be a big draw in this small Alaskan town.

"Nope. And I don't plan to either. I'm not looking to settle down," he said in a brusque tone. "I like being single and unattached."

Maggie felt as if her eyes might bulge out of her head. "Really?" The question slipped out of her mouth before she could rein it back in.

Hmm. How had the women in this town allowed an Alaskan hottie like Finn to stay single? It seemed as if he would be a hot commodity in Love.

"Is that so hard to believe?" he asked, raising his eyebrows in her direction.

"I'm just surprised. You have so much to offer. And the way you are with Oliver and Aidan, I can't imagine you not being a father."

"Some things just aren't meant to be. I don't relish

that type of responsibility." The tone of Finn's voice sounded resigned.

"Is this about your father and the way he walked away from you and Declan?" she asked, shocking herself by asking the probing question. If Finn hadn't been a childhood pal she would never have dared. But she couldn't deny her curiosity about his family. Back in the day Maggie had been envious of his picture-perfect family. How had it all fallen apart so disastrously?

Finn looked startled for a moment. His jaw looked tight. He seemed to be struggling to answer her question. "Yes, I'm sure that has something to do with it. I've always been aware that it comes with a huge responsibility—one I'm not looking to assume."

The forlorn tone of his voice made her wish she hadn't been so nosy. No doubt she'd stirred up painful issues from the past. How would she like it if someone started probing into Sam's death? All of her family skeletons would come tumbling out of the closet. If the truth came out it was possible the townsfolk would treat her like a pariah, just as they had in Boston. She shivered at the thought, knowing Oliver's future could be compromised if that happened.

"I'm sorry for asking. It's none of my business," she said in a brisk tone. "I didn't mean to open any old wounds."

Finn met her gaze from across the room. "You should know something. In a town this small you'll probably hear it at some point." Finn let out a ragged sigh. "My mother was killed accidentally by my father. They were fooling around in our backyard one night with a shotgun and they'd had a few too many beers. One minute they were joking around and the next moment the gun went off by mistake. She died right there at our house."

Maggie felt as if she'd been holding her breath the entire time Finn spoke. His revelation was shocking. Her heart broke for him and the entire O'Rourke family and all they'd lost because of such a senseless tragedy. This whole time she'd been wondering about the adult version of Finn and trying to pinpoint all the ways in which he had changed. Now it was all clear. The little boy who had been filled with such mischief and light and heart didn't exist anymore. Trauma had forever changed him.

"Finn! I'm so sorry you went through that heartache. I know how much you loved her. She was such a beautiful and kindhearted woman. And she loved you all so very much."

Maggie remembered Finn's mother. Cindy O'Rourke. She'd been gentle and kind and her laughter had filled up their home. She had baked peanut butter cookies and made rocky-road fudge. Maggie had often wished that her own mother could be a lot more like Finn's.

Maggie had experienced her own share of hard knocks in her childhood, but nothing like what Finn had endured. Loss after loss after loss. It was heartbreaking.

Finn broke eye contact with her and looked down at one of the boxes. "It was unimaginable. Truth to be told, losing her almost broke me. It definitely tore my father apart. He ran away from Love because he couldn't bear the pain of what happened. He ended up spending some time in jail for petty crimes." His voice softened. "I understand why he left us and why everything in his life fell apart. It still hurts though. To lose our mother and then our father—" His voice became clogged with emotion. He cleared his throat, then began to rummage around in one of the boxes.

"And then your grandfather passed," she said as memories of a sweet, round-faced man with a deep-throated laugh sprang to mind. Killian O'Rourke had been such a source of pride and inspiration. Everyone in town had adored him.

"Yep. It was like a domino effect," he said, his head still bowed. "That one nearly did me in. When he got sick I left town. It was too painful for me to stay here and watch him die."

Maggie felt a chill sweep across her back. She felt Finn's agony acutely. It was infused in his voice. It radiated from every pore on his body. "It must have been agonizing."

"And Declan had to deal with yet another loss. Only this time he was all alone. I bailed on him."

Maggie didn't know what to say to try to make it all better. Maggie had been widowed before she even turned thirty years old. So she kept quiet, knowing all too well some things couldn't be fixed or smoothed over.

"So you see, Maggie, I'm the last person who feels the need to get married and raise a family. I'm not exactly dependable. When Declan really needed me to help care for our grandfather, I was exploring Yosemite and backpacking my way through life." He let out a bitter-sounding laugh. "Nice, huh?"

She shrugged. "You did what you had to do to get by. No one has the right to judge you."

"Except myself," he muttered.

They both settled back into digging through inventory. Maggie tried to focus on the job at hand, but her thoughts kept veering back toward Finn and his tragic past. It made her chest tighten to imagine the ten-year-old Finn having to deal with such horror. Sam's death had put Oliver through the wringer, but Maggie had been by his side steadfastly throughout the whole ordeal.

She now knew a whole lot more about the adult Finn than she'd ever imagined discovering. He associated family with loss. Heartache. He hadn't put it into those exact words, but she sensed he was still running away. Although he was physically here in his hometown, he was afraid to attach himself to anything significant.

She didn't blame him. Finn O'Rourke had lost a lot in his life. She imagined he didn't have a whole lot more to give of his heart. She knew a little bit about how it felt to feel so beaten down and jaded. Frankly it was a shame. Because something told her that like his childhood self, Finn had more heart and soul in his little pinkie than most had in their entire bodies.

Chapter Six

Finn loved Christmas. It was one of his most closely kept secrets. Although he hardly ever showed it, on the inside he was like a little kid bubbling with excitement in anticipation of the holiday season. Finn wasn't sure even Declan knew how much he loved the hoopla and the decorations and the feeling of goodwill toward humankind. As a man who had messed up a lot in his life, he deeply appreciated the idea of reconciliation at Christmas. It was the perfect time to embrace the Lord. He was deeply flawed, but God still loved him.

Ever since he was a kid, Finn had thought it was pretty awesome how he could mess up a million times, but it didn't change the way God felt about him.

I have loved thee with an everlasting love. The verse from Jeremiah had always stuck with him. It had sustained him during the worst moments of his life. Even though he was a sinner, he still had God's love.

And way past the age when kids believed in Santa, Finn had continued to believe with all his might. Although most people thought a little bit of the Christmas spirit evaporated once the secret of Santa was revealed, it had only made Finn more convinced of the beauty of this sacred time of year. Along with God, people were at the heart of Christmas.

On his way into town this morning he had cranked up the radio and rocked out to Christmas music. It didn't matter that he couldn't carry a tune. He could still belt out the lyrics about someone rocking around the Christmas tree. As he stood outside Keepsakes he stopped and looked up at the faded sign and the ramshackle exterior.

It needed to be spruced up before the snow came. The local weatherman had been reporting about a snowstorm hitting town in a few days. He made a mental note to mention it to Maggie and to remind her to stock up on household food and supplies by tomorrow.

Finn let himself into the shop with the key Maggie had given him. He flicked on the lights and surveyed the store. Although progress had been made, there was still lots to do before Keepsakes could open its doors. After about ten minutes of rooting around the shop, Finn heard the front door being opened. Maggie came in bundled up in a burgundy-colored coat and matching scarf. Both looked as if they'd seen better days.

"Good morning," Finn said.

Maggie grimaced. "'Morning."

Her normally friendly greeting was missing in action today. He studied her closely. Her eyes were red and it was clear to Finn she had been crying.

Finn frowned. "Wasn't today Oliver's first day of kindergarten?" Shouldn't Maggie be smiling?

Maggie nodded but didn't say a word.

"How'd it go?" he asked. He was being polite by asking. Finn didn't want to know the answer. He could see it all over her face. The idea of Maggie crying made him feel incredibly uncomfortable. He wouldn't know what to do to console her if she broke down in front of him. And the idea of her being in pain made his chest tighten uncomfortably.

"Terrible," she said in a mournful voice. "I walked him inside like all of the other parents and we stayed until the teacher rang the start of school bell." Maggie heaved out a deep breath. "Then all of the kids started waving to their parents and some of them were having a hard time saying goodbye."

Finn winced. "Let me guess. Oliver cried?"

Maggie put her hands on her hips. "No, he didn't cry. Nor did he wave or run up to me and give me a farewell kiss. He smiled, then turned around and joined the others for singing class. Seems they're putting on a little Christmas show and Oliver needs to memorize four songs."

"That's great. Sounds like he took to it like a duck to water."

Maggie nodded, lips trembling. "Yep. Oliver came through it with flying colors. Not so sure about Mom though. I feel as if I've been run over by a Mack truck. It's rough being the new kid in town."

"Maggie, you're going to be fine. Everyone knows that the first day at a new school is harder on the parents than on the kids. It's a thing."

"It is? You're not pulling my leg are you?" she asked in a wary voice.

"Of course not. And you should be really proud of yourself. Oliver is a well-adjusted kid, despite having lost a parent. Do you have any idea how incredible that is?"

A smile slowly crept across Maggie's face. Although he thought she was beautiful, a full-fledged smile transformed her into someone extraordinary. "It is pretty amazing now that you mention it." She ran her hand through her shoulder-length chestnut-colored hair and beamed.

"Hey! Look over there!" Finn cried out, pointing at a spot near the front counter.

"What is it?" Maggie asking, whipping around to see what had gotten Finn so excited.

"There's a clear spot over there. Can you believe it?" Finn asked.

Maggie shook her head and giggled. "It was bound to happen one of these days."

Finn enjoyed making Maggie laugh. He liked watching the way her eyes crinkled and her nose scrunched up. He had a feeling she had no idea of her appeal.

It was sad that they'd resorted to this type of humor, Finn realized, but seeing a clear spot in the shop felt like spectacular news. They had been working nonstop for days to get rid of heaps of items they'd deemed as trash and get the shop in decent order. For the first time it seemed as if there was a light at the end of the tunnel. With the holidays rapidly approaching, they needed to open as soon as possible.

A sudden knocking on the door halted their conversation.

Maggie looked at him with big eyes. "Someone's at the door."

He held his finger up to his lips.

"Hello," a masculine voice called out. "Maggie. Maggie Richards. It's Dwight. I've come to welcome you back to Love and to offer my condolences about Tobias."

Finn let out a soft groan and rolled his eyes.

"Dwight? As in Dwight Lewis?" she asked in a loud whisper. "The kid who used to wear bow ties and Bermuda shorts?"

"One and the same," Finn answered with a grin. "And in case you were wondering, he still wears those bow ties." Maggie started laughing, then clapped her hand over her mouth to silence herself.

It felt nice to have history with Maggie. They could share little inside jokes and memories from a time when his life had been idyllic.

Maggie scrunched up her nose. "Didn't we have a nickname for him?"

Finn smirked. "I think we had a few. If you open that door and let him in, word will travel around Love as fast as quicksilver about the state of things inside this shop."

Maggie's eyes widened. "That could be very bad for business," Maggie whispered. Finn wanted to laugh out loud at the outraged expression on her face, but he knew Dwight might hear him. Finn wouldn't be surprised if the town treasurer had his ear pressed up against the door.

"I'm heading over to the Moose to visit my fiancée,

so if you'd like to come say hello I'll be across the way," Dwight said in a raised voice.

Finn rolled his eyes at Dwight's mention of his fiancée, Marta. Dwight had been single for a long time, but the minute he fell in love and got engaged to the chef at the Moose Café, he'd decided not to let anyone forget his status. For more reasons than one it rubbed Finn the wrong way.

Maggie and Finn huddled next to each other, waiting for any slight sound to indicate Dwight's presence. They were standing so close to one another Finn could see the golden flecks in her green eyes. He could also hear the shallow sound of her breathing.

"Do you think he's gone?" Maggie whispered. She was leaning so close to him her hair swung against his cheek.

"Mmm-hmm," Finn said, feeling slightly bowled over by his close proximity to Maggie. She smelled like flowers. Roses, perhaps. It was a heady scent. She was all kinds of pretty. There was an air of grace about her, he thought. She was soft and feminine, but there was strength at her core, even if she didn't seem to realize it. Losing a husband so tragically and at such a young age could harden a person, Finn imagined. But she didn't seem bitter at all. Maggie seemed determined to find stability for Oliver and to make the best of her inheritance from Tobias.

"I think we're safe," Finn said, reluctantly moving away from Maggie.

"Phew," Maggie said, swiping the back of her hand across her forehead. "He was persistent."

Finn made a face. "He's town treasurer now. You really have no idea. On any given day he's like a dog with a bone."

Maggie put her hands on her hips. "How about we stop for lunch and then tackle the shelving areas?"

"Sounds good, but I don't think we should go over to the Moose Café," Finn said, wiggling his eyebrows. "Unless of course you want Dwight to know we were here the whole time."

She made a face. "No way. We can just pick up some sandwiches at the deli."

Finn cast his gaze around the store. With every hour he and Maggie spent clearing up the place, Finn was moving one step closer to his dream—co-ownership of O'Rourke Charters. Working side by side with his younger brother would be life altering. Finn still had a lot of work to do in order to show Declan he was back in Love for good.

Now that the shelves had been cleaned and polished, Keepsakes was beginning to look like an actual store. For the first time, Maggie knew they were out of the woods. She sat down on a crate and breathed in a deep sigh of relief. She cracked open a diet soda and raised it up in the air in a celebratory gesture. Although she never would have said it out loud to Finn, there had been many times when she'd doubted they would reach their goal in time. It wasn't very often she felt proud of herself, but in this moment she felt as if she had accomplished something monumental.

God was good. He had led her to this moment, and

even though she had wavered many times in her faith, He was still showing her His grace.

A few minutes earlier Finn had volunteered to pick up Oliver at the bus stop then take him over to the Moose Café for a treat. Knowing Oliver would get a kick out of seeing Finn and spending time with him, Maggie agreed. Plus, it would give her the time to sit for a little bit and soak in the knowledge of the path she was about to walk down. Store ownership.

An hour later Finn walked through the door with her son at his side. Oliver had a chocolate mustache, no doubt from indulging in hot chocolate with Finn.

"Hey, buddy! How was your first day at school?" Maggie asked.

"It was great," Oliver said. "I made a lot of new friends."

Maggie felt as if her heart might jump out of her chest. All of her fears had been rattling around in her head. And now here Oliver stood looking as happy as a clam. She let out the breath she'd been holding ever since dropping Oliver off at school. Suddenly, all was right with her world.

Oliver began chattering about the goings-on at school.

"We were talking about Christmas at school. There's a big cookie exchange coming up where everyone makes cookies and then swaps so you end up with a whole bunch of cool holiday cookies. Aidan asked me to go sledding with him, so I also need a sled. And we need a Christmas tree, Mom. Everyone else has one." Oliver looked at her with pleading eyes.

"Oh, really now?" Maggie asked in a teasing voice. It tickled her to think her son was already in the thick of things with his classmates.

"Can we? Can we, please?" he begged, crossing his hands in front of him.

She leaned down and pressed a kiss against his temple. "Yes, my sweet. We most definitely can. I know the perfect place at home we can put it." There was no way Maggie could say no to the excitement bubbling up inside her son. She'd made a promise to herself. She was going to embrace Christmas and all it had to offer, if only to see the joy reflected in her son's eyes. Christmas trees! Sledding at Deer Run Lake! Participating in the town's Christmas cookie exchange. She was all in.

"Can you come and help us pick out a tree, Finn?" Oliver asked. There was something about the look emanating from Oliver's eyes that sent out warning signals. He was getting attached.

Finn playfully bowed to Oliver. "It would be my pleasure, Sir Oliver," he said in an exaggerated English accent.

Oliver giggled. "You sound funny." He turned toward Maggie. "When can we go to find the tree?"

"How about if we head over there tomorrow night?" Maggie suggested. "I have a few things to take care of around here. And I still have to figure out dinner."

"How does that sound, Finn?" Oliver asked, turning back toward Finn.

"Sounds like a plan," he said, holding up his palm so Oliver could high-five him. "I don't know if you heard," he said, bending down and speaking in a low voice to Oliver, "but I'm the best tree hunter in all of Alaska."

"Cool! We're going to get the best tree ever," Oliver said, his face lit up with excitement.

Maggie watched the interplay between Finn and Oliver. There was no doubt about it. They were getting along like a house on fire. Oliver was blossoming right before her eyes. And it had everything to do with Finn. She should know. He'd done the same thing for her when she was ten years old.

"Finn, can I talk to you for a second?" She waved him over so Oliver wouldn't overhear their conversation.

"Sure thing." He walked over to her, his eyes alight with curiosity. "What's up?"

"You asked me the other day about watching Oliver after school so I can focus on the shop."

Finn waved his hand at her. "Forget it. I know you weren't keen on the idea."

"I was being unreasonable," she admitted, feeling very humbled. Her overprotectiveness toward Oliver had clouded her judgment. "Your offer to watch Oliver was very generous. Honestly, he's crazy about you."

"So? Did you change your mind? Are you taking me up on my offer?"

She took a deep breath. "Yes, I am, if it's still on the table."

Finn graced her with a wide grin. "Hey! That's great. Of course it is."

Maggie chewed on her lip. "I think I was just worried he might get too attached to you. Oliver isn't just looking for a father figure, Finn. He's actually looking

for a father. I just don't want him to get hurt or confused along the way."

"No worries, Mags. We're buddies," Finn assured
her. "Surely that can't be a bad thing."

"No, that's not a bad thing," Maggie said, her eyes
drifting back toward her son. He was still looking at
Finn as if he was the greatest thing since sliced bread.

She felt relieved about the childcare situation being
resolved. Finn had been right. It was the perfect solu-
tion. *Unless of course Oliver decides he wants Finn to
be more than a buddy*, Maggie thought. She knew her
son hadn't given up on the idea of finding a father here
in Alaska. Something told her Finn would be at the top
of Oliver's list.

Finn headed over to the Moose Café as soon as he
and Maggie decided to call it day at Keepsakes. Since
Annie was working late at the library, Declan had invited him to dinner. It would be nice to get together with
his brother and talk over a good meal. It had been far
too long since they'd spent downtime together.

The jangling of the bell heralded his arrival inside the
eatery. Finn smiled as he looked around the place. Every
time he walked in, it seemed as if Hazel and Cameron
had added even more festive decorations. Yes, indeed.
It was beginning to look a lot like Christmas.

"Hey, Finn. Are you looking for a table?" Sophie
asked, coming up behind him.

"I'm looking for Declan. He's supposed to be meeting me here for an early dinner," Finn said.

"I haven't seen him yet, but I can find a table for the

two of you," she said, waving him to follow after her. Finn trailed after her and sat down once Sophie placed two menus on a table set up for two.

"As soon as I spot him, I'll send him over."

"Thanks, Soph. Tell Noah I said hello, okay?"

At the sound of her husband's name, Sophie lit up like sunshine. "I sure will, Finn."

Sophie was a newlywed, having married Noah Catalano, a private investigator, after a whirlwind courtship. Folks in town were still grappling with Sophie's hidden identity as an heiress to a coffee empire. Her bank balance wasn't important. Sophie was well loved in this town.

Yep. Single folks were dropping like flies in this town, which meant it was only a matter of time until someone asked him about his status. An unattached male in Love who wasn't signed up for Operation Love was akin to a Bigfoot sighting. Everyone wanted the happy ending tied up with a big fancy bow.

"Where has Maggie been hiding?" Hazel asked with her hands on her hips as she made a sudden appearance at his table.

"Well, hello to you too, Hazel," Finn said in a dry tone.

She placed her hand on his shoulder. "Sorry, Finn. I don't know where my manners went," Hazel said in an apologetic tone. "How are things going over at the shop? Rumor has it you're helping out over there."

So far Finn had discussed his inheritance from Tobias only with his brother and Maggie. He knew Love like the back of his hand. Once word got out, he wouldn't have a moment's rest answering questions from the townsfolk. He loved Hazel, but for the time being he wasn't disclosing the particular reasons why he was helping out at Keepsakes. He was keeping his mouth shut about Tobias's will and his eyes on the prize.

"There's a lot of work to do. For the most part Maggie's been working to get the shop in running order." Finn made a face. "Don't repeat this, Hazel, but Tobias left that shop in really bad shape."

Hazel scratched her chin. "That's hard to fathom," Hazel said. "Tobias was such a meticulous person. I imagine he was overwhelmed when he got sick and made the decision to close up the store. It wasn't until much later that he took me into his confidence about his illness." She made a tutting sound. "It's frustrating because I can't imagine a single person in this town who wouldn't have helped out if he'd said one word about the shop."

Finn shrugged. "I was pretty close to Tobias and he didn't mention the shop, although he talked about Maggie all the time. He used to show me pictures of her and Oliver. It was pretty obvious he was crazy about them."

Hazel nodded. "He sure was. Tobias always hoped Maggie would make it back here." She shook her head. "I think he was a little brokenhearted he didn't see her again before he passed."

Finn straightened in his chair. "Hazel, could you make sure not to share that sentiment with Maggie? I think it would really wound her to know that particular bit of information."

"Me and my big mouth. I didn't mean it as a criticism

of Maggie," Hazel said. "Tobias was such a kind and generous man. His death is such a big loss to this town."

"I know." Finn reached out and clasped Hazel's hand in his own. "I just want to make sure Maggie doesn't get hurt."

"You and Maggie have been spending a lot of time together," Hazel said, sending him a pointed look. "Don't think people haven't noticed. Are the two of you going to be the next It couple in this town?"

Finn waved his hand at her. "You've got it all wrong, Hazel. There's nothing romantic going on. We're just friends, just like back in the day."

"Finn is antiromance. Didn't you know, Hazel?" Declan came striding up to Finn's table. Obviously he'd heard the tail end of their conversation. Declan put his hands around Hazel's waist and placed a kiss on her cheek before sitting down across from Finn. Finn had to smile. As always, his brother knew how to make an entrance.

"Is that true, Finn?" Hazel barked. "There are lots of pretty gals here in Love looking for a God-fearing, handsome man like yourself." She tapped her fingers against her breastbone. "Look at me! I never imagined I'd be a newlywed at my age, but God has a plan for all of us. I learned not to question His timing."

Finn glared at Declan. "I'm not against romance." He shrugged. "I just don't want to settle down. It's not for me."

"Humph. And why not? It's not as if you haven't backpacked around the country and sowed your wild oats," Hazel muttered. "What are you waiting for? An engraved invitation to court someone?"

Declan sat back in his seat and chuckled. "That's what I'd like to know. With Annie expecting, it would be nice for my kids to have some cousins to rip and run with. At this rate they'll have to play among themselves."

Kids? A wife? Finn felt a twisting sensation in his stomach. Those weren't on his agenda. Not now. Not ever. Just the thought of it made him feel as if he couldn't breathe. It would be too much pressure for him. He'd promised God a long time ago he wouldn't even try to go down that road. That was his punishment for what he'd done to his family. A solitary life free of familial responsibilities. He had already destroyed one family. He wasn't going to risk tearing apart another one.

"We haven't seen hide nor hair of Maggie. Dwight was here asking about her. He said he went over to the shop but she didn't answer the door." Hazel tutted. "Poor thing is probably working herself to death. Maggie needs to get reacquainted with this town and the folks who live here."

As if from out of nowhere, Jasper sidled up to their table and stood next to Hazel. "Are you talking about Maggie? I keep wondering where she's hiding herself. Let's get her involved in town events. Maybe she'll want to join the PTA or the town council," Jasper suggested. "We actually have a position on the town council opening up in a few weeks."

Declan and Finn locked gazes. They both began to chuckle.

"What's so funny?" Jasper asked, his expression one of irritation. "Being on the town council is an honor."

"Those aren't exactly rip-roaring good times," Finn drawled.

"We don't want her to think Love is a snoozefest," Declan added. "How about the Christmas cookie exchange or the Deer Run Lake skating party?"

Finn snapped his fingers. "And what about the choral group who sings carols door-to-door?" Finn wanted Maggie and Oliver to experience the best of Love. The happier they were, the more likely they would stay in Love long-term. He felt a bit badly about not encouraging Maggie to participate more in town events. He had been so eager to finish work on the shop so he could collect his inheritance and buy into O'Rourke Charters. He'd lost sight of the fact that Maggie needed to be exposed to a wide range of things in Love.

"Ooh," Hazel exclaimed. "I just found out there's a holiday mixer for Operation Love participants. Maggie's been invited even though she hasn't officially signed up yet for the program. There's still a female shortage in this town, so nobody minds bending the rules and allowing her to attend." Hazel jabbed Jasper in the side. "Something tells me the men of Love will be vying for Maggie. She's a good-looking woman."

"Sure is," Jasper said with enthusiasm. "I don't want to be indiscreet, but a few men have already asked about her." Jasper wiggled his eyebrows. "That holiday mixer would be great for Maggie to meet some eligible men." He rubbed his hands together. "Another Operation Love success story in the making."

"Don't count your chickens before they hatch," Hazel said, her lips pursed.

"What are you talking about?" Jasper asked. He puffed his chest out. "I'm an expert on the program and matchmaking in general. You should know that Maggie Richards will be the perfect partner for some fella in this town."

Finn felt himself grinding his teeth. He counted to ten slowly in his head. All this talk of Maggie and Operation Love was irritating. Finn didn't like the way Hazel was eyeballing him either. She was studying him like he was a biology exam.

"Let's leave these young 'uns alone so they can look at the menu. Come help me in the kitchen," Hazel said to Jasper in a blustery voice as she pulled her husband away from the table.

Finn felt himself tensing up. The idea of men fighting over Maggie wasn't a pleasant one. And even though Jasper wasn't giving up any names, Finn wanted to know who was asking about Maggie. There were a few men in Love who shouldn't even think about approaching Maggie. He could think of at least five off the top of his head.

Humph! They didn't even know her. Her likes and dislikes. Her favorite color. How she liked to spend her downtime. Did they even know she had a son?

"What's wrong? You look bent out of shape."

"Nothing. I just don't like the idea of some of these guys swarming over Maggie like bees to honey," he muttered.

Declan looked at Finn from over his menu. "Why

not? If she finds the man of her dreams, won't it be a good thing?"

Finn clenched his jaw. A good thing? Yes. Maggie deserved to find happiness, but he couldn't deny the unsettled feeling in the pit of his stomach. She was a single mother and a widow who had lived through tragedy. She put on a brave front, but she was vulnerable in many ways. If Finn had anything to say about it, he wasn't going to let Maggie pair up with just anybody. The guy needed to be as solid as a rock.

Sophie appeared with two glasses of ice water and placed them down on the table. "I'll be back in a jiffy to take your order."

Finn looked down at the menu, studiously avoiding his brother's gaze. After what seemed like an eternity, he looked across at Declan, who was still staring at him. Finn let out an exaggerated sigh. "Just say it. I know you want to tell me something, hence the Darth Vader stare."

Declan's lips twitched at the Star Wars mention. "I know you're into Maggie. You can't fool me, Finn." The look on Declan's face spoke volumes. Sometimes his brother could be like a dog with a bone. He wasn't going to back down on this topic.

"Of course I like her. She's beautiful. And super sweet. You should see her with Oliver." He shook his head. "She's wonderful. But honestly, I'm not looking to romance her. I don't do serious. And I'm certainly not looking for a ready-made family." He let out a harsh laugh. "Seriously? Can you see me with a wife and a kid?"

Declan wasn't laughing. He narrowed his gaze and studied Finn. "Honestly, I can easily picture it, Finn. You're a good, honest man. You've made some missteps in the past, but who hasn't? You've really stepped up in the last year and come into your own. I think it's time you stopped beating yourself up about it."

Finn felt a huge lump in his throat. Declan's vote of confidence meant the world to him. But there were things his younger brother didn't know. He had no clue about Finn's role in their mother's death and the gradual dissolution of their family unit. Finn's worst fear was Declan finding out and casting Finn out of his life for good. Without Declan and Annie, Finn wouldn't have a family. He would be completely alone.

As Sophie came back to the table to take their order, Finn could barely concentrate on ordering his meal. Fear had grabbed hold of him.

All of these years he'd managed to keep his guilty secret from Declan. A shudder went down his back at the prospect of Declan finding out the truth about him being responsible for the accident that had killed their mother and the brutal aftermath—his father leaving the family and Killian's death some years later. Finn had lost most of the people in his life he held dear. He didn't think he would able to bear it if he lost Declan too.

Chapter Seven

As Maggie peered around the thick brown paper still covering the storefront window she saw the gently falling snow. It looked so beautiful and serene. It truly resembled one of those idyllic images from a calendar. From this vantage point she could see the Moose Café, as well as other shops on Jarvis Street. She was counting down the days until they could rip down the paper and Keepsakes could join the other businesses in their holiday cheer.

Maggie couldn't remember a time in her life when she had worked so hard toward a goal. With the exception of her first few weeks as a mother to a newborn and the shocking circumstances of Sam's death, getting Keepsakes ready for business had become the most difficult endeavor in her life.

On the bright side, the shop was taking shape, and she could see all of the possibilities laid out before her. She had put aside items that she wanted to showcase in the front windows as a holiday display.

Day by day her friendship with Finn was strengthening. They were beginning to fall into old, familiar rhythms. He made her laugh with his corny jokes and she delighted him with tales of Oliver's antics. They chuckled over their childhood escapades and the fanciful dreams of their youth. It was nice to be friends with a man without romance messing things up. Although Finn was appealing on so many levels, Maggie couldn't see herself romantically involved with anyone. Sam had done enough damage to her heart to last a lifetime.

"You wanted to be a crime fighter," Finn had reminded her earlier that morning. "I vividly recall you talking about wearing a red cape and riding to the rescue."

"You wanted to be a pilot by day," Maggie recounted with a chuckle. "And a pizza maker by night."

"Sounds reasonable to me. Flying and pizza. Two of the finest things in life." Finn shook his head. "Such goals we had."

"We wanted to rule the world," Maggie said in a wistful tone.

They had been so innocent back then. At ten years old it had been easy to believe in happy endings and dreams come true. Both she and Finn had been exposed to darkness in their lives. Despite her belief that God hadn't been by her side through the tough times, Maggie now knew it wasn't true. He had seen her through the worst of it, and through Uncle Tobias, God had shown her grace and pointed her in a new direction.

Life tended to provide reality checks along the way. And then she'd had to switch up her dreams, Maggie realized, as she looked around the store. This place was her new dream. A feeling of gratitude threatened to overwhelm her. She'd never really allowed herself to imagine owning anything with such potential. Things were coming together.

She and Finn had arranged for a garbage disposal company to pick up the items in the shop deemed to be trash. At Finn's suggestion, they also had a pile of items they were donating to a charitable organization benefiting the homeless. In a few days a crew was coming in to help them give the place a top-to-bottom cleaning. They had a lot of work to do before then.

"Hey, Maggie." Finn's voice interrupted her thoughts. "I've been thinking. You've been working so hard here at the shop. It hasn't given you much time for socializing."

Maggie swung her gaze up from the front counter. Her mind felt blank. What was Finn talking about? The Operation Love campaign?

"Socializing?" she asked. It had been so long it felt like a foreign concept.

Finn chuckled. "Yes. As in getting to know the townsfolk. You're going to need their friendship and goodwill once the store opens. I'm one hundred percent certain you'll get their support, but it would be nice to have some established ties."

Maggie shrugged. "Well, I have you and Hazel. And there's Jasper and Declan." She was counting on her fingers. "And Ruby and Aidan."

Finn looked at her without saying a word. He didn't have to speak. His expression said it all.

She bit her lip. The town of Love was a small hamlet,

but even she knew her numbers were pitiful. When was the last time she'd made an actual friend? Or ventured out of her comfort zone? Moving to Alaska had been a huge leap of faith, but it would be meaningless if she failed to connect with the townsfolk who lived here.

So much had been lost over the years, including her ability to connect with people.

"I did a little brainstorming last night about the grand opening. I think we should think big." He spread his arms wide. "Huge. We could make up flyers and host a holiday party here with eggnog and red velvet cake and lots of party favors."

Maggie smiled. She loved Finn's enthusiasm. Although it was crystal clear he was working with her in order to get his inheritance, he never hesitated to go the extra mile. He had a great attitude. It was no small wonder Oliver thought he'd hung the moon.

"That's a great idea," Maggie said. She rubbed her hands together. "Who doesn't adore eggnog?"

Finn looked at his watch. "I can man the store if you want to head over to the meeting for the carol singers. Pastor Jack would love to have you. They're meeting in the fellowship hall at the church at noon." He wagged his eyebrows at her. "I seem to remember you singing at church when we were kids, and I hear they're looking for a soprano."

"I do enjoy singing. It's been a while though," she said in a soft voice.

So many things had been watered down over the years due to Sam's problems. She had distanced herself from her church community due to the shame she'd felt after his death. How could she have walked into church after all the media attention and finger-pointing?

And she knew she hadn't really grieved Sam in the proper way. Her anger and shock and embarrassment hadn't allowed her to fully mourn the man she'd loved but hadn't ever really known.

"I imagine it's like riding a sled down a mountain." Finn's eyes twinkled as he mentioned their favorite childhood pastime. "Something you never quite forget how to do."

Finn was right. She loved singing, especially in a group setting. Why had she given up something that gave her so much joy and brought her closer to God?

A sheepish feeling swept over her. Why was she feeling so reluctant to make friends in Love? She had been excited about making those connections, but now she felt nervous. There had been so much rejection back in Boston. Maggie almost felt wary of opening herself up to being hurt again by judgment and derision. It had been an incredibly painful experience to be shunned.

"Are you sure you can hold down the fort by yourself?" she asked. A part of her wanted him to tell her he couldn't handle dealing with the store by himself. That would give her a way out. Truthfully, the shop had become something of a cocoon for her. She spent all of her days at Keepsakes and her evenings were occupied by Oliver.

"I can definitely handle it, Mags. As they say, Rome wasn't built in a day. We're making great progress here. This place is starting to look terrific. Take a moment to stop and smell the forget-me-nots." Forget-me-nots were the official state flower of Alaska.

Although Finn's voice had a teasing tone, Maggie could sense he was serious. It hit her all at once. Finn cared about her. Despite all the years of separation, he still wanted the best for her. It made her feel all warm and fuzzy inside.

"Okay. Why not? I'm going to go meet up with the choral group." She sat down on a chair and pulled on her warm, fuzzy boots. She had splurged yesterday and bought a pair of Hazel's Alaskan Lovely boots. Maggie wasn't used to having new things. For so long she'd scrimped and saved to try to keep a roof over her family's heads and to see to Oliver's needs. Now, with this inheritance, she didn't have to constantly worry about every dime. She had even purchased a few items to put under the tree for Oliver. She couldn't wait to see the look on her son's face when he unwrapped the toboggan.

Finn nodded his approval. "Have a good time. I'll meet Oliver at the bus stop. No worries."

Maggie put her coat and hat on, then reached in her purse for her mittens. "I'll see you later." Strangely enough she felt like a child venturing out into the big bad world all by her lonesome.

"Hold on a minute," Finn called out. He walked up to her and reached out to zip up her jacket so her neck wasn't exposed. She looked up into his sea green eyes. "There. It's cold out there. We wouldn't want you to get sick." They locked gazes, and Finn smiled. Maggie felt the oddest sensation as she gazed into Finn's eyes.

Butterflies soared in her belly. For a second she felt her palms moisten.

She shook off the feeling. Maybe she was coming down with something. Maggie gave herself a mental pep talk and headed toward the back entrance to Keepsakes. She turned around and waved at Finn, who was standing there staring at her as if she was a baby chick leaving the nest.

Step out of your comfort zone. Believe in yourself! Nothing ventured, nothing gained. She repeated these phrases in her head as she pushed open the back door and headed out into the wintry morning.

Although Maggie was trying to be brave, a part of her wanted to turn right back around and hide herself away in the shop. But she knew Finn wouldn't let her get away with it. And the truth was, she didn't want to disappoint him.

Finn didn't quite know what to do with himself while Maggie was gone. Although he kept himself busy hauling things outside to the back of the shop and doing a little online research about pricing for items, his mind kept wandering to Maggie. Was she having a good time with the choir? Had they welcomed her with open arms?

Maggie had looked so unsure of herself and nervous. He'd been torn between encouraging her and protecting her. He didn't remember her being so anxious. But they'd been ten years old. So much had happened in both of their lives since then.

By the time Oliver got off the school bus, Maggie still hadn't returned from her choir meeting. Oliver almost chatted his ear off, telling Finn stories about his kindergarten buddies and their antics. Finn loved seeing the boy's excitement and the innocent way in which he viewed the world around him. He felt a sudden need to make sure Oliver didn't lose his sense of wonder. Finn wanted to wrap a protective blanket around the kid so he wouldn't get jaded or hurt by life.

Stop it! You're not his father, he chided himself. *It's not your job to worry about Oliver. He has a mother, and no doubt he'll have a father soon.*

Operation Love tended to work pretty fast in Finn's estimation. Before too long Maggie would be paired up with one of the numerous men who'd signed up for the matchmaking program. Finn shouldn't feel annoyed about it, but he did. It was silly. Just because he'd decided not to enroll in the program didn't mean Maggie couldn't make the most of it. And if she did get married, they could still be friends. Somehow that thought didn't do anything to make him feel any better.

Maggie and Oliver were top-notch. He let out a sigh. A man would have to be a fool not to see it.

Lord, please let Maggie find what she's looking for here in Love. If she somehow finds it through the Operation Love program, then so be it. I know Oliver wants a father, but I want Maggie to find her own happiness. She's been through a lot.

The door to the shop swung open and Maggie came bustling in, carrying a plastic tin. Oliver ran toward her and hugged her tightly around the waist.

"What a nice greeting. Seems like you missed me," Maggie said.

Oliver nodded and pressed his face against her. "Did you bring something for me?" Oliver asked, sniffing the tin.

"I brought some monkey bread. It's delicious," Maggie said. "You're going to love it."

"So, don't keep us in suspense. How was it?" Finn asked. He'd been on pins and needles since she'd left.

The smile on Maggie's face threatened to overtake her entire face. "It was a lot of fun. I'm sorry I took so long, but I went for a hot chocolate with Ruby and some other ladies."

A sense of relief flooded him. "That's great. Who did you hang out with?"

She scrunched up her face. "Let's see. There was Paige and Grace and a Gretchen. I like them all a lot. And it felt so good to sing again."

"That's some fine company you were keeping. Those ladies are wonderful."

Oliver tugged at Maggie's sleeve. "Mom, you said we could go get the tree tonight. Remember?" The look on Oliver's face was hesitant, as if he was bracing for Maggie to say she'd forgotten all about it.

"Of course I do," Maggie said. She leaned down and pressed a kiss on Oliver's temple. "I've been looking forward to it all day."

"Mom, you're getting mushy again," Oliver said, dramatically swiping his hand across his forehead.

"Does tonight still work for you, Finn?" Maggie asked.

"It sure does," he said. "Why don't we grab something to eat across the street then head over to the town green? It's pizza night at the Moose Café. They'll be making ten different types of pizza. You name it. Pineapple pizza. Meatball pizza. Reindeer pizza. And the always popular, Heart of Love pizza. It has five kinds of cheese and it is literally the most delicious thing I've ever tasted in my life." Finn rubbed his stomach and made a funny face, much to Oliver's delight.

"Sounds like an artery-clogging experience," Maggie said, chuckling behind her hand.

"I know you love pizza," Finn said, shooting her a knowing look. "Come on. Admit it. You're going to have five slices of the artery-clogging, five-cheese pizza."

Oliver began giggling. "She usually just has two."

"Just you wait and see," Finn said with a wink. "She's going to devour this pizza."

"Can we go now?" Oliver asked, rubbing his stomach.

"Let me just make sure all of these boxes have been broken down and then we can head over," Finn said, his eyes scanning the shop. "I can't believe how good the place looks."

Maggie folded her arms across her chest and looked around her. "No, Finn. It looks great. I'm astounded by how nicely everything is shaping up. I think tomorrow I'm going to get started on the window display."

After a delicious pizza dinner at the Moose Café, Finn walked over to the town green with Oliver. Maggie drove her car down Jarvis Street and found a spot close to the tree stand in case they found a tree and needed to strap it on top to take it home.

Powdery snow was falling all around them. Oliver

was running around with his head tilted back so he could catch snowflakes in his mouth. It was like a beautiful postcard of an Alaskan Christmas scene. Being here with Maggie and Oliver felt like a sweet privilege.

Thank You, Lord, for this beautiful moment. I'd almost forgotten the simple joy of looking for the perfect Christmas tree.

It had been far too long since Finn had participated in such a heartwarming outing. For far too many Christmases he had been roaming around the United States, far away from his hometown. He'd missed out on a lot of moments. This year would be very different. He was going to soak up as much as he could of the holiday festivities here in Love. And he was going to live in the moment and enjoy every single second of it.

There was a multitude of Christmas trees lined up in rows. Trees of all shapes and sizes. Finn inhaled deeply. The scent was one of his favorites. It brought to mind everything he loved about the season.

"See anything you like?" Finn asked Oliver.

When Oliver reached up and grabbed hold of his hand, a funny sensation spread across Finn's chest. It was such a simple thing, yet it made him feel like a rock star. He couldn't deny the raw emotions it brought up inside him. Suddenly, someone needed him. Was this what it felt like to be a father? If so, it was incredible. Oliver made him realize that he wasn't such a black sheep after all. He may have messed up a bunch of times, but in Oliver's eyes, he was still a pretty good guy. And that meant the world to Finn.

As they walked from tree to tree, Finn found his gaze

straying to Maggie. Her tender interactions with Oliver demonstrated her loving nature. She was a wonderful mother. Every child should be so grateful as to have a mother like Maggie.

Joy hummed and pulsed in the air. Everything felt pure and serene. If there was such a thing as a perfect moment in time, Finn knew this was it.

Oliver began jumping up and down. He was pointing at a medium-sized pine tree. "Hey, guys. Isn't that a great tree?"

In Finn's opinion it looked a bit lopsided, but he wasn't going to put a damper on Oliver's enthusiasm. If he wanted this slightly imperfect tree, then so be it.

Finn reached out and wrapped his hand around the base and then shook it. "It seems really solid."

"This is it!" Oliver said. "That's our tree."

"Are you sure?" Maggie asked. "Once we buy it and strap it to the top of the car, that's it. We're not coming back for another one."

"I'm absolutely one million percent sure," Oliver said, his expression solemn.

"Well, it doesn't get any better than that," Finn said, sharing a bemused look with Maggie. "Let's buy it."

Maggie began to dig around in her purse. Finn reached out and placed a gentle hand on her wrist. "The tree is on me. Consider it my welcome-to-Love gift to you and Oliver."

"That's not necessary, Finn. You're already doing so much to help out our family."

"Maggie, let me do this. Trust me. Tobias's inheritance is going to change my life in unimaginable ways."

He ran a hand over his face. "I'm not sure I've wrapped my head around Tobias's generosity."

Maggie nodded. "I know the feeling. Oliver and I have been so incredibly blessed. Not only by Uncle Tobias, but by your friendship and the generosity of the people here in town. Jasper. Hazel. Ruby. This town really is something special."

Finn walked away from Oliver and Maggie, making his way toward the tent so he could purchase Oliver's tree.

"Hey, Al. I think we've decided on a tree," Finn said, greeting Alan Pendergast, the owner of the tree stand. He reached out and handed Al a wad of cash.

"Hey, Finn. Good to see you. Which tree are you looking at buying?"

Finn turned around and pointed toward Maggie and Oliver. "The one right there beside the woman and the little boy."

Al nodded. "So is that Tobias's niece?"

"Yes, that's Maggie," Finn said. "And her son, Oliver. They're living out at Tobias's place."

Al let out a laugh. "I remember her as a little tyke. Tobias sure loved that girl."

Finn nodded. Tobias had been a devoted uncle to Maggie, even though a huge geographical distance separated them. He couldn't count the number of times Tobias had pulled out photos and letters from Maggie. Finn always had the impression Tobias viewed Maggie as his honorary daughter.

"He sure did," Finn acknowledged. "She's going to

do him proud by running Keepsakes and carrying on his legacy here in Love."

Al jerked his head in the direction of Maggie and Oliver. "Who's the guy standing with them?" Al let out a chuckle. "You can't even turn your back in this town without someone trying to steal your lady."

Finn quickly turned around. From this distance he couldn't be certain, but it looked like Hank Jeffries had sidled up to Maggie in his absence. He had his palm up waiting for Oliver to give him a high five. Finn recognized his height and broad shoulders, as well as the red-and-black lumberjack coat he always wore. A feeling of irritation washed over him. Hank was a fireman. Ladies loved firemen, although for some inexplicable reason, Hank was still single and available. And according to the rumor mill, he was looking to settle down.

Finn clenched his teeth. Hank was well regarded and a genuinely nice guy. It wasn't any of his business who courted Maggie or tried to make friends with Oliver. After all, hadn't Oliver spilled the beans about wanting to find a father in Love? Hank would fit the bill just fine, he imagined. He was heroic and strong and he didn't run away when things became too overwhelming.

Finn turned his back on the sight of Maggie, Hank and Oliver. The sudden appearance of Hank reminded him of his own unworthiness. He felt like a deflated balloon. Maggie and Hank made sense. He was the very definition of *reliable*. Steadfast. No doubt the whole town of Love would cheer them on.

"She's not my lady," he said in a curt voice to Al.

"Really? The two of you aren't the latest couple from

Jasper's program?" Al asked, his brow furrowed in confusion.

For some reason, Al's question pricked at Finn. This whole evening had felt idyllic until reality had slapped him in the face. Hank's sudden appearance had been a jolt to the system, serving to remind him in no uncertain terms of his own inadequacy. He wasn't the type of man who could give Maggie and Oliver what they truly needed and deserved—stability.

"We're not dating," Finn snapped. "Maybe I should put a sticky note on my forehead saying we're just friends."

Al held up his hands. "Okay. I didn't mean to get you all riled up. It's just that you three look like a family. And Declan settled down last year. Figured you might want to follow his lead."

He blew out a frustrated breath. "How many times do I have to tell everyone in this town? I'm not interested in Operation Love or getting married or starting a family. I don't want to be a father or a husband. I'm doing perfectly fine all by myself."

The moment the words tumbled off his tongue, Finn felt like a jerk. Al's hurt expression spoke volumes. Once again, Finn O'Rourke had messed up.

As Finn turned around to leave, he met Maggie's shocked gaze. She was standing directly behind him with wide eyes. He felt a sinking sensation in the pit of his stomach. There was no question about it. Maggie had overheard his rant.

He let out a ragged sigh. So much for their perfect evening.

Chapter Eight

Maggie's cheeks felt flushed as she stood awkwardly in the entranceway to the tent. Maggie had never heard such anger in Finn's voice. It had surprised her. For the most part, he always seemed so upbeat and content. And this evening had been so idyllic up to this point.

A thick tension hung in the air. She had no idea what to say to fill up the silence.

She'd been standing with Oliver when Hank Jeffries had come over and introduced himself to them. It had quickly become clear he had a romantic interest in her. Although he was handsome and friendly, Maggie had felt slightly uncomfortable. She'd been out of the dating game for quite some time. Even before she'd met Sam, Maggie had always felt awkward about dating. Clearly, nothing had changed.

On the pretext of asking Finn a question about the tree, Maggie had beat a fast path toward the tent. In the process, she'd stumbled upon a very revealing conversation.

Finn stood by silently, seemingly speechless.

"You must be Maggie." The older man came toward her and stuck out his hand. "I'm Al Pendergast. This is my Christmas tree stand. You probably don't remember me, but your uncle was a dear friend of mine. I met you once or twice when you were knee-high to a grasshopper."

Maggie shook his hand and shot him a shaky smile. "It's a pleasure to meet you again. You've got some beautiful trees here. My son is delighted."

"You sure know how to make an old man smile. I pride myself on top-quality Christmas trees." Al grinned. "Why don't we head back over to the trees and I'll wrap it up for you?"

As they walked back toward Oliver and the tree, Maggie couldn't help but notice Hank had disappeared. She felt a twinge of guilt about not being more receptive to him, but he'd caught her off guard. She probably didn't have to worry about him asking her out. She'd acted like a skittish newborn colt.

Mr. Pendergast placed the tree in a machine that wrapped it up in netting. Finn easily picked up the tree and strapped it to the top of Maggie's car.

"I'll follow behind the two of you in my car," Finn said. He'd barely said two words since she had surprised him in the tent. Maggie wasn't sure if he was embarrassed or annoyed with her for overhearing him. Either way, it felt awkward.

"Can I go in Finn's car?" Oliver asked, crossing his hands prayerfully in front of him.

Maggie tugged at his sleeve. "No, Oliver," she said in a sharp voice. "You're driving with me."

Ignoring her son's pout, Maggie got in the driver's seat and revved the engine. Oliver was becoming entirely too enamored with Finn. Perhaps she needed to sit him down for a little talk about their friendship. Oliver wasn't shy about telling her he wanted her to find him a forever father. It wasn't too much of a leap for Oliver to imagine Finn in that role.

Lord, please protect my son. His heart is as wide and open as the great outdoors. I don't want him to get his feelings hurt. He's already been through so much.

As she drove home, Finn's words played back in her mind. *I'm doing perfectly fine all by myself.*

Maggie didn't know why it bothered her so much to have overheard Finn's harsh-sounding words directed at Mr. Pendergast. It wasn't any of her business if he wasn't a proponent of the town mayor's matchmaking program. To be honest, neither was she. So what if he didn't want a wife and kids? It really didn't concern her. Finn was her friend, not a prospective mate. Because she felt so comfortable around him and she knew Oliver loved him, Maggie had allowed Finn a place in her life that wasn't strictly in the friendship zone.

If she was being really honest with herself, there was chemistry between her and Finn. The extensive amount of time she'd been spending in Finn's company had created a bond between them. But Maggie wasn't looking for love. She was seeking stability and a solid foundation. Although Oliver wanted a father, Maggie didn't need a man to help her give Oliver a bright future. She was fully capable of doing it on her own.

Finn had made things crystal clear about his wants and needs. He didn't need to spell it out any further. Finn liked having a solitary life. And he wasn't interested in changing. For the first time Maggie realized Finn had layers like an onion. On the surface he was jovial and full of zest, but underneath he was struggling with something. Maggie was certain of it. She knew from her own experience what it looked like when a person was keeping secrets.

Maggie had her own problems to deal with as a single mother making a new life for herself. Although Finn was a good friend, it wasn't her place to try to solve his issues. She already had her hands full trying to make sure Oliver was healthy and happy. The wounds from Sam's death were still so fresh.

When they arrived home, Finn carried the tree into the house, with a little assistance from Oliver. Maggie couldn't help but smile at the sight of her son carrying the tail end of the tree. He really wanted to be a mini version of Finn.

Once inside the house, Maggie directed Finn and Oliver toward the living room. Finn placed the tree in the tree stand right in front of their big bay window. She knew it would look spectacular when it was fully decked out with ornaments, lights and a shiny gold star on top. She could imagine it all, including gaily wrapped presents sitting under the tree.

"Thanks for helping us pick a tree, Finn," Oliver said

with a wide grin. "And you were right. You are the best tree hunter in town. Maybe in all of Alaska."

"Thanks, kiddo," Finn said. "It was a real honor to be asked to join you and your mother. Finding the perfect Christmas tree is epic. You made my day!"

"You made mine too. It wouldn't have been half as fun without you." Oliver looked up at him. "I know you're super busy, but I really want to go flying with you."

The wistful tone in Oliver's voice made Maggie weak in the knees. One word from Finn and her son would be crushed. She found herself holding her breath. *Please, Finn,* she prayed. *Don't break his heart.*

"We can go on Saturday morning, bright and early." He locked gazes with Maggie. "Does that sound all right?"

There was no way in the world Maggie could say no, even if she'd wanted to. Oliver was looking at her with an expression of such hope shining forth in his eyes. "Sounds like a plan. I'll head into the store and set up the window display while you boys have your adventure."

Oliver let out a roar of approval. "This is the best day ever!" he yelled.

"I think it's time to head upstairs so you can get ready for a bath and bedtime. Say good-night to Finn," Maggie instructed.

"'Night, Finn," Oliver said, looking up at him with a shy expression etched on his face.

"See you later, gator," Finn said, tousling Oliver's hair.

"In a while, crocodile," Oliver shouted out as he raced toward the stairs.

Once they were alone, Finn walked over toward her. His hands were stuffed in his pockets and he had a sheepish expression etched on his face.

"About what you overheard back there at the tree stand," Finn began. "I don't want you to think I'm against people finding love or anything. I think it's great. And I'm not against Jasper's program. It's just not for me."

Maggie held up her hands. "You don't need to explain anything to me. I hope you don't think I would judge you for your opinions."

Finn quirked his mouth. "Maggie, I'm a single guy in a town full of bachelors who are all tripping over themselves to find a woman to settle down with." He shook his head. "I'm a bit of an anomaly."

"Glad to see nothing's changed since we were kids," Maggie teased. "You always were an outlier."

"That's a nice way of putting it." Finn chuckled. "Good night, Mags. I'll see you at the shop tomorrow."

Maggie saw Finn to the door and waved as he drove off into the dark Alaskan night. As soon as she shut the door, she leaned against it and pondered the events of the last few hours. Despite the slight tension at the Christmas tree stand, it had been an enjoyable evening, full of laughter, fellowship and discoveries. Oliver had thoroughly enjoyed himself with Finn. And Maggie had felt grateful for adult companionship.

If Maggie's past hadn't been filled with heartache and betrayal, she might be in a position to test the waters. Based on her research, Operation Love was a resounding success. Even Finn's own brother had found love through the program with Annie, who ran the Free Library in town. According to Ruby, Annie had come to Love in order to run the new library, then fallen in love with Declan O'Rourke, the pilot who had flown her to town. And her new friend Grace had met the sheriff of Love, Boone Prescott, through Jasper's matchmaking program as well. The list of successful matches was quite lengthy.

She'd heard so many romantic stories about Operation Love and people finding their true north. The truth was, Maggie was no longer looking for a fairy tale. She would be content to raise Oliver in a house filled with love and faith. She'd had her one love in a lifetime. Before everything had gone so horribly wrong, she and Sam had been a love story. Over time their marriage had buckled under the strain, but they had been a love match when they'd pledged forever to one another. Despite what people said, Maggie wasn't sure a person got two bites of the apple.

No matter how much she cared for Finn, there was no sense in hoping for something that would never happen. She and Finn actually had a similar outlook on romance. Finn was closed off to relationships and commitment. Maggie had been burned in the not-so-distant past by a husband who hadn't been on the same page with her or the lifestyle she wanted to lead. Right before her very eyes Sam had changed. And she hadn't been any the wiser until the bottom fell out of their world. There was no way she was going to set herself up for any more heartache. As it was, Sam's duplicity had brought her to his knees.

It was wise to keep Finn strictly in the friend zone and keep her heart strictly out-of-bounds.

Maggie's a friend and nothing more. Over and over again, Finn repeated the phrase until he felt certain it was seared into his brain.

He'd made a mistake by becoming too attached to the beautiful single mother and her adorable son. He didn't have any romantic feelings toward Maggie, but he felt protective of her and Oliver. Being such a big part of their new lives in Love was dangerous to his decision not to form any lasting attachments. The night of the tree-hunting expedition, Finn had vowed to maintain a healthy distance from Oliver and Maggie. The lines were getting a little blurred, especially when people like Al started linking him romantically with Maggie.

Finn let out a snort. The tree stand owner had actually thought they were a couple. Finn stuffed down the little burst of joy he felt at being linked with his childhood friend.

Maintaining a distance from the Richards family was a difficult proposition since he was working with Maggie by day in the shop, then watching Oliver each weekday afternoon and some weekends. It seemed as if he couldn't manage to detach himself from their lives. And it was wreaking havoc on him. Despite his best intentions, Finn was finding it impossible to stay away from Oliver and his mother. He kept reminding himself that he didn't want to get too tangled up in their lives. Somewhere down the line Maggie might fall for someone here in town, and it wouldn't be fair to the man in question if Oliver's feelings toward Finn continued to blossom. It was very clear how Oliver felt about him—it was a very strong case of hero worship. Because Oliver was fatherless, Finn knew it was very possible Oliver had sought him out as a father figure.

Finn let out a sigh. The last thing he ever wanted to do was hurt Oliver. In some ways he reminded Finn of himself as a kid. Funny. Wise. And incredibly vulnerable. Finn could sense a lot behind Oliver's eyes.

For today he wasn't going to worry about building a little bit of a protective fire wall between them. Today was all about providing a wonderful flying experience for Oliver.

Finn O'Rourke didn't renege on promises. Especially not to six-year-old boys who made him feel as if he'd hung the sun, the stars and the moon.

Finn felt almost as excited as Oliver as he arrived at the airport hangar. He had arisen early this morning, bursting with enthusiasm about taking Oliver on a flying adventure. He stood outside and gazed out over Kachemak Bay. He couldn't have asked for better flying weather if he'd put in a special order for it.

As soon as he saw Oliver and Maggie walking toward him, Finn felt adrenaline racing through his veins. It was always like this before he flew—excitement pulsing through his body. It was a rush, pure and simple. The thrill of a lifetime.

Finn knew the moment Oliver saw him standing in the airport hangar. He started running toward him at breakneck speed, leaving Maggie in the dust.

"Welcome to O'Rourke Charters. Thanks for choosing to fly with us today, Oliver." Finn gestured toward the plane. "Please step inside and make yourself comfortable."

"Awesome!" Oliver practically tripped over himself making his way to Finn's side.

Finn placed his hand on Oliver's shoulder. "I think you're forgetting something," Finn said, jutting his chin in Maggie's direction. Finn could read Maggie's face like a book. She was fretting over her decision to let Oliver fly with him.

"'Bye, Mom," Oliver said, rushing toward Maggie and hugging her tightly around the waist. "Thanks for letting me do this."

Maggie's expression instantly transformed. She was smiling down at Oliver with an expression of joy etched on her face. Oliver's happiness was contagious.

"Be safe up there," she called out to them.

"Always," Finn said with a wave before helping Oliver into the plane. Oliver's eyes widened once he realized his seat was right in the cockpit next to Finn's seat. Once Finn was seated in the cockpit, he set Oliver up with a headset so they could talk over the roar of the plane.

"Up to the wild blue yonder," Finn called out as he worked the controls and began to ascend into the sky.

Oliver repeated Finn's words, reminding him of the way he and Declan had always recited those same words—their grandfather's mantra.

Once they were up in the air at a decent altitude, Finn began pointing out landmarks.

"This is my grandfather's plane," Finn explained.

"I fixed it up a few months ago so it runs perfectly. It's called the *Killian* after him. He taught both Finn and me to fly on this plane."

"Wow. It must be old," Oliver said.

Finn let out a throaty laugh. "It is. We don't fly any customers in this plane. We reserve it for very special people."

"Like me?" Oliver asked, his grin threatening to split his face wide open.

"Exactly like you, Oliver." Finn turned toward Oliver. There was something about this kid that endeared him to Finn. He was curious and sweet and he had a zest for life unlike anyone else. Finn cared about Oliver in a way he couldn't even explain to himself. The kid brought up feelings inside him he'd never felt before. He could safely say he would take a bullet for Oliver.

"Look out the window! Do you see those trees covered with snow? That's Nottingham Woods."

"It looks so small from up here. Jasper said it was huge!" Oliver said, wrinkling his nose as he peered out the window. "They don't really look like trees."

"It's actually a really big forest like Jasper said. When we were kids my brother and I used to go cave hunting with our friends, the Prescott brothers. And guess what? Your mom came, too, whenever she visited."

"She did? Aw, man. I've never been in a cave," Oliver said in an awestruck voice. "Will you take me sometime?"

Finn grinned. Oliver was a boy after his own heart. He would have asked the same thing when he was Oliver's age. "If your mom says it's all right, I sure can," Finn said with a wink.

Finn steered the plane to the left, dipping it down low at an angle to give Oliver a thrill. Oliver let out a whoop of excitement. A few minutes later Finn spotted the glistening waters of Kachemak Bay down below. Patches of white reflected ice chunks on the surface. Finn loved looking down at the body of water. Its raw power was awe inspiring.

"Do you know what that is down below?" Finn asked.

"Kachemak Bay," Oliver said without hesitation.

"You're saying it perfectly. It takes most folks a while to learn the right way to pronounce it."

"Mom taught me on the ride over," Oliver said, his voice full of pride. Finn felt a little hitch in his heart at the sight of Maggie's son sitting beside him in the plane. He must be a resilient kid to have lost his father not so long ago and still be able to greet the world with a smile and optimism. He prayed Oliver's future wouldn't be hampered by the loss of his father. He knew all too well how those wounds festered.

As Finn made a final loop around Love, he looked out across the landscape of the hometown he adored. For so long he'd denied the pull of this town and what it meant to him. He glanced over at Oliver. He was sitting quietly, gazing out over the horizon with a look of satisfaction etched on his features.

"We're about to go into our descent and head back to the hangar," Finn announced. Truthfully, he could hang out in the sky for hours, but he knew Maggie needed him at the store for a few hours. He wanted to check out her window display and slap some red paint on the sign outside the shop. In a few days, the shop would be ready for the grand opening.

After landing the plane, Finn led Oliver inside the airplane hangar. A quick glance at his watch showed he was still within the time frame he'd promised Maggie. They could have a quick snack then head over to the shop.

"Hey, Oliver. There's a fridge out back. Why don't you go grab a juice box or some chocolate milk? I've got some stashed back there."

"Okay," Oliver said in an agreeable voice before dashing off.

Declan was sitting at his desk poring over some paperwork. He swung his gaze up and focused on Finn.

"You're pretty crazy about Oliver, huh?" Declan asked. His blue eyes were twinkling with interest.

"He's a great kid," he said in a curt voice. Declan wasn't fooling him. He knew his brother was trying to stir something up about his feelings for Maggie and Oliver.

"You and Maggie seemed to have picked up right where you left off all those years ago. I remember the way the two of you were as thick as thieves."

"We're friends. You can tell Annie not to start planning a wedding shower," he said in a dry voice.

"Why would she do that? Word around town is that Hank Jeffries is interested in Maggie." Declan flashed him a smug look. "They're going out on a date."

Whoosh. Finn felt a jolt pass through him. Maggie

hadn't mentioned anything about Hank or going out on a date. It wasn't as if she owed him that type of information, but Finn felt a little bit of a shock. He spent most days working side by side with Maggie. Why hadn't she confided in him about Hank?

"Seems to me if you're interested in Maggie you ought to speak up before she's taken." Although Declan tossed the words out casually, Finn knew his brother was trying to prod him into action.

"What part of *not interested* don't you understand? We're friends, just like in the old days."

"You two are like peanut butter and jelly. You finish each other's sentences. That's how it was when I met Annie. For a while I resisted what it meant. Don't be so stubborn, Finn. You're blocking your blessings."

"I'm not like you, Declan. Not everyone embraces marriage and kids with open arms. I knew at a young age I wasn't going to get the white picket fence and the house full of kids."

Declan frowned. "I understand, to an extent. Before I met Annie I had my doubts about happily-ever-after, but loving her helped me make peace with the past. I hope you see how it's possible. I'm living proof."

Just then Oliver came back into the room, juggling two small boxes of chocolate milk in one hand and some apple slices in the other. He grinned at Finn. "Look what I found. I got one for both of us." He handed a chocolate milk to Finn.

"We'll pick this conversation up later," Declan said, shooting Finn a glance filled with meaning. He smiled at Oliver. "I'm glad you had a good time today, Oliver."

"It was awesome," Oliver said. "Finn's the best pilot in all of Alaska."

Finn threw his head back and laughed. It was nice to hear a vote of confidence from Oliver.

The corners of Declan's mouth were twitching with mirth. "I see I'm outnumbered," he said.

Declan leaned across his desk and said in a loud whisper, "Don't tell Finn I said so, but I agree with you." He looked at his watch. "I better head off toward the pier. I'm making a run to Homer."

After Declan's departure, Finn sat down with Oliver so they could enjoy their chocolate milk and apple slices.

"So, what do you have planned for later on?" Finn asked. "Anything exciting for the weekend?"

He wrinkled his nose. "Mom has a date tonight," Oliver said in a soft voice. "I'm hanging out at Aidan's house."

Finn tensed up. Clearly, Declan's information had been correct. Even Oliver knew about it.

He made sure his voice sounded cheery. "Really? Well, that's nice."

Oliver frowned at him. "Do you really think so?"

"Sure. Why not?" he asked, hoping to inject a little positivity into the situation. Clearly, Oliver wasn't impressed with his mother's plans.

"Because if Mom goes out with this guy then they might get married. Aidan told me all about the Operation Love program," Oliver said, his voice trailing off. He bit his lip and stared at Finn with a troubled expression.

"Would that be such a bad thing?" Finn asked.

"Yes, it would," he said in a raised voice. "I don't want her to marry just anybody, Finn." His hazel eyes pooled with tears. "I want her to marry you."

Chapter Nine

Maggie cranked up the holiday music and did a little dance around the shop. Everything looked wonderful. The shelves had been painted a pristine white. The hardwood floors were glistening. Trash had been cleared. The charity organization had stopped by to pick up the donations. Stock had been delivered.

They still had some work to do, but it was night and day from when they had opened up the door and come face-to-face with a shop in disarray. That day Maggie had prayed for wisdom and strength to go the distance. With the help of Finn, Maggie was a few steps away from her goal of opening up Keepsakes in time for the holiday season.

Becoming a part of the fabric of this quaint town involved being seen. She didn't want to be a shadow anymore. It was the Christmas season. Celebrating the birth of Jesus meant rejoicing with your community. Locking herself away meant Maggie was living in fear. She didn't want to do that anymore. Not for herself or

Oliver. She wanted to embrace everything this town had to offer.

Maggie reached out and ripped down the brown paper from the windows. As light flowed into the shop, Maggie felt as if she was being embraced. She hoped Finn didn't mind her taking down the brown paper without him. She'd been caught up in a moment. It had felt right.

While she was setting up the window display, numerous townsfolk passed by the store. They smiled and waved at her. Some gave her the thumbs-up sign as they watched her set up the miniature Christmas tree and the snow globes on one side and the twinkling reindeer and the smiling snowman alongside it. Once she was done she stepped outside and surveyed it.

The sound of clapping interrupted her perusal of the display. Finn and Oliver were walking down Jarvis Street and straight toward her. Finn was clapping enthusiastically.

"It looks great!" Finn stepped closer to the windows and examined her displays. "I'd say this is the best holiday display on Jarvis Street."

"What do you think, Oliver?" Maggie asked. "Do you give it a thumbs-up?"

Oliver shrugged and pushed snow around on the pavement with the tip of his boot.

"What's wrong?" Maggie asked, reaching out and tilting Oliver's chin up so she could look him in the eyes.

"Nothing," he said in a short tone.

Maggie raised her eyebrows at Finn. She turned back

to Oliver. "Well, you better tell that to your lip. It's sticking out like a sore thumb."

Oliver rolled his eyes and walked past them, entering Keepsakes without saying anything further. Maggie's first instinct was to read Oliver the riot act. She had no intention of raising a brat with no manners.

"That attitude is unacceptable." Maggie frowned. "Did something happen?"

Finn sighed. "We had a great time flying, but afterward he began talking about your date."

Maggie gulped. "My date? With Hank?"

"Yes. He's not too keen on the idea of it."

"It's nothing. We met up at the mixer for Operation Love. We're just going out to dinner."

Finn held up his hands. "You don't need to explain a single thing to me."

Maggie's face crumpled. "I should cancel it. It's not worth upsetting Oliver."

"No, you shouldn't. Oliver is six. He's bound to try to put his foot down from time to time. I think they call it pushing the boundaries. If you let him have his way with this, you're going to create a little tyrant." He folded his arms across his chest. "Do you want that?"

"No, Finn. I most certainly do not. But maybe it's too soon," Maggie said. "He's just a little boy grappling with adult issues."

"Only you know if that's true or not. Keep in mind why you came here to Love in the first place. To change your life. You can't do that by standing on the sidelines."

"I need to talk to him, but what should I say?" Maggie asked. As a mother, Maggie usually had all the answers or at least a hunch about how to handle things. At the moment she felt clueless. She trusted Finn's advice.

"I think you should simply tell him you're meeting up with Hank because you're trying to get to know people here in town. Don't make too much of it. If you do, he'll pick up on it and freak out again."

Maggie nodded. "You're right. That sounds good."

On impulse, Maggie threw herself against Finn's chest and wrapped her arms around him. "Thank you. Not just for this advice, but for treating Oliver so well. Even though he's in a bit of a funk right now, you made one of his dreams come true today."

When she released Finn, she noticed he was staring at her with a strange expression on his face.

"What is it?" she asked, wondering if she had something stuck between her teeth.

"Nothing. It's just that…you're a fantastic mom, Maggie. Oliver is very blessed to have you. He's not at the age where he's going to say it to you in so many words, but I know he feels it. Right here," Finn said, tapping his chest.

Tears stung Maggie's eyes. The compliment from Finn meant everything to her. Every day she got up in the morning and put one foot in front of the other trying to do her best for her son. It felt gratifying to hear she was doing a decent job of it.

"Thanks, Finn," she said, her voice choked with emotion. She prayed he was right about Oliver. She felt so tangled up inside knowing he was upset about her plans with Hank. Being a mother wasn't all peaches and cream. It was tough, never-ending work, and not for the faint of heart.

She took a deep breath as she headed back into the store. Somehow she was going to have to find a way to talk to Oliver about her date with Hank.

Finn knew he'd blown things earlier with Oliver. When Oliver had spoken to him after their flying adventure about Maggie's date with Hank, he'd been completely shocked by Oliver's comment about wanting him to become his father. The comment had come out of the blue. In response, Finn had stumbled and fumbled, without a clue as to how to compassionately deal with a six-year-old boy's tender wishes.

He had deliberately withheld that information from Maggie when she'd asked him about what was bothering Oliver. It would have been awkward to tell her what Oliver had said to him. He was still wrapping his head around the six-year-old's comment and annoyed at himself for not responding well to it.

When he walked back into Keepsakes, Finn looked around the store for Oliver. He was sitting down at a little table Maggie had set up for him. His elbows were on the table and his head was slumped down next to the coloring book. He wasn't coloring or doing anything other than brooding.

A quick glance in Maggie's direction showed her distress over the situation. He didn't know what was bothering him more. Oliver's upset mood or Maggie's frame of mind.

"Hey, Oliver," he called out. "I've been thinking about something."

Oliver barely moved. "What?" he mumbled.

"You still haven't met Boomer yet," he said in a casual tone.

Oliver quickly raised his head up. His face lit up like a Christmas tree. "Boomer? Your dog?" Oliver's voice was infused with unbridled enthusiasm.

Finn folded his arms across his chest and rocked back on his heels. "Yep. One and the same. He gets really lonely when I'm away from the house. And he really likes visitors, especially kids your age."

"Really? Do you think he would like me?" Oliver asked. He stood up from his chair and walked over to Finn.

Finn laughed out loud. "Are you kidding me? He'd be crazy about you."

Finn shot a glance at Maggie, asking her a question with his eyes. She nodded discreetly.

"If you and your mom aren't busy tomorrow you could swing by and meet Boomer. If you think it's something you'd like to do, that is," Finn said.

"Yes! Of course I would," Oliver shouted, wrapping his arms around Finn's waist and giving him a tight bear hug. Finn felt certain no one had ever showered him with such enthusiasm in his entire life.

Maggie shook her head as Finn received the hug of a lifetime. Finn could see the relief etched on her face. It made him feel like a million dollars to have been able to do something to soothe Oliver and to provide comfort to Maggie. It troubled him a little bit. Never in his life had he felt this way before. And he didn't quite understand it. Why did it mean so much to him to be there for Maggie and Oliver?

He related to Oliver because of his own experience with grief as a child. In some way he felt as if he was uniquely qualified to help the boy navigate his way through his terrible loss and the newness of their life in Alaska. If things had been different, it would have been a privilege to be Oliver's father.

He would have to settle for being Oliver's best friend and ally.

Pink and purple streaks of color stretched across the horizon. The rugged mountains popped out at her, making Maggie feel as if she could simply reach out her hands and touch them. If Maggie was a painter this would be her muse—the magnificent Alaskan landscape.

"Oh, it's a beautiful Alaskan morning," Maggie said as she gazed out of her bedroom window. "God sure did create a masterpiece when He made Alaska," she gushed. With each and every day, Maggie fell more in love with her surroundings.

Last night had been a pleasant evening in Hank's company. Although he had been a true gentleman, Maggie knew they could never be more than friends. Hank was looking for a wife and she didn't want to waste any more of his time. It wouldn't be fair to allow him to pursue her when she knew how she felt.

She heard Oliver rumbling around in his bedroom. Although they were due at church service in an hour,

Maggie suspected Oliver had arisen early due to his excitement over meeting Boomer today at Finn's place. He had talked her ear off about it all afternoon and into the evening. She was fairly certain he had dreamed about it last night, she thought with a grin. That's how it should be for little boys. Dogs and trains and pilots with sparkling green eyes and infectious smiles.

Her bedroom door burst open and Oliver stood in the doorway. "Is it time to go to Finn's house yet?"

"Not yet. We have church service first," Maggie reminded him. "Don't you remember? I'm singing with the choral group."

"Aw," Oliver said in a loud voice.

Maggie didn't say a word. She sent her son a look full of reproach.

"Okay, I'm going to go get dressed for church," Oliver said in a chirpy voice. "I can't wait to hear you sing."

By the time they left the house half an hour later, both were dressed to impress. Maggie was wearing a cranberry-colored dress she had recently bought here in town. She had some high-heeled nude shoes she was going to slip on once they'd made it to the church. Navigating the snowy Alaskan weather dictated the use of boots. Oliver had put on his best pair of slacks and a dark blue sweater. She couldn't get over how mature he looked all of a sudden. He'd grown by leaps and bounds during the last year.

Maggie enjoyed singing with the choir at church. Oliver sat in the front pew and clapped along to the music. Although they were invited to stick around after the service for a pancake breakfast, Oliver practically dragged her out of the church.

"Oliver, we need to go change out of our church clothes," Maggie said.

"Why can't we just wear what we have on?" he asked with a groan.

"You can't play with Boomer in your Sunday best."

Oliver grumbled all the way back to the house, then practically vaulted out of the car when they reached home. Maggie was certain she'd never seen her son move so fast. It was as if his feet were on fire. She quickly changed into a pair of jeans and an oatmeal-colored sweater. Oliver was waiting impatiently for her at the door, wearing a sweatshirt and a pair of dark jeans.

Maggie drove the truck to town, navigating the snow-packed roads with a measure of confidence she hadn't felt when she'd first arrived in town. At moments like this Maggie wondered what Uncle Tobias might think of what she was doing. Hopefully, he would feel proud of his niece and the steps she had taken toward rebuilding her life.

As soon as the small, log-cabin house came into view on Swan Hollow Road, Maggie let out an admiring sigh. Finn's house was lovely. It was rustic and cozy. The house was nestled in a wooded area with a clear view of Kachemak Bay. It seemed like the perfect setting for Finn.

Right after they drove up, Finn walked outside, accompanied by a sweet-faced dog with black-and-white fur. He had a fancy red collar around his neck with rhinestones on it. Maggie thought he looked adorable.

"Boomer!" Oliver called out as he jumped out of the truck. The medium-sized dog ran toward Oliver and jumped up on him, knocking him to the snow.

"Down, Boomer!" Finn ordered. "Sorry about that. He tends to wear his heart on his sleeve."

"It's okay. He's just being friendly," Oliver said. "I don't mind."

Boomer's tail was wagging ferociously. Oliver threw his arms around Boomer and hugged him. He began to pat him in a loving manner. Maggie had the feeling Oliver would once again be asking for a dog of his own.

"We got a present for you, Boomer." Oliver looked at Maggie. "Do you have it, Mom?"

"Sure thing," Maggie said, digging in her purse. "Here it is. Make sure it's okay with Finn to give it to him." She handed Oliver a bone wrapped up in a big red bow.

"Thanks, guys. He'll love it." He waved them toward the house. "Why don't we go inside and you can give Boomer the bone?"

Finn ushered Maggie and Oliver inside his home. The smell of pine wafted in the air. Another smell assailed her senses. It smelled like freshly baked cookies.

"Your house is lovely, Finn," Maggie remarked, looking around her at the sparsely decorated home.

"Thanks. I'm renting it, but I'm hoping to buy it from the owner. I'm crossing my fingers it all works out when I become co-owner of O'Rourke Charters. I'll be making a full-time income then and I can qualify for a mortgage."

Maggie's heart warmed at the possibility of Finn finally staking roots in Love. For so long he had been running away from making his hometown his permanent home. Surely this was a sign of growth and change, Maggie thought.

"Excellent," she said. "Inheriting Uncle Tobias's house has allowed us to own our first home. We were always renters. It's an amazing feeling."

Finn clapped his hands together. "Hey, can I offer either of you something to drink? Hot chocolate? Tea? Cider? I have some cookies in the kitchen. They just came out of the oven."

"Mmm. They smell good," Oliver said, following Finn toward the kitchen.

"Aren't you full of surprises?" Maggie murmured as she spotted several racks of cookies sitting on the stove.

"I like baking," Finn said with a shrug. "Especially Christmas cookies. Most of these are for the winter carnival tomorrow night. Help yourselves though. I made more than enough."

Maggie reached over and grabbed a gingerbread cookie dusted with sprinkles. She took a bite and let out a sound of appreciation. "Hey, you're good at this, O'Rourke. This is delicious."

"Finn is good at everything," Oliver crowed, biting into a cookie.

Finn tousled his head and said, "Thanks, buddy."

"I guess I better pick up some snow pants for us so we can go to the winter carnival," Maggie said, thankful

Finn had mentioned the event. With everything going on with the shop, Maggie had completely forgotten all about it.

As Maggie sipped a cup of green tea and watched the interplay between Oliver, Finn and Boomer, she couldn't help but wonder about Finn's determination to stay single and unattached. This house seemed perfect for a family. It was way too big for one person, and Finn seemed to enjoy being with people. He wasn't exactly a loner.

Finn O'Rourke was an enigma. The more she thought she knew the man, the more she realized there were many aspects of him she might never be able to fully understand.

Having company over at his house wasn't something Finn was used to. He hadn't lived here very long, but lately the place had begun to feel like home. Inspired by Maggie and Oliver's Christmas tree, he'd even put up one of his own—a lovely balsam fir that towered over him. He still needed to buy a few more pieces of furniture. At the moment his style was minimalist. But, considering where he'd been little more than a year ago, his current situation represented major progress.

There was something so comfortable about having Maggie and Oliver hanging out with him at his house. It felt like family had stopped by. Conversation flowed easily. Finn didn't feel he had to do anything special to entertain them. Oliver was enamored with Boomer. And Boomer seemed to have fallen in love with Oliver as soon as he gave him the juicy bone.

"I think it's time I took Boomer for a walk. Want to come along, Oliver?" Finn asked.

"Sure thing," Oliver said, jumping up from his seat.

Finn hoped Maggie wouldn't offer to come along on the walk. Although he always enjoyed being around her, there were some things he needed to set straight with Oliver. And he thought it might be best if she wasn't around.

"I think I'll stay here and read the paper. Grace has an interesting article in here about making an Alaska bucket list," Maggie said, her nose buried in the local gazette.

Finn led Oliver out through the back door. He handed him Boomer's leash and began walking toward the woods.

In his excitement, Boomer was pulling at his leash.

"Don't let him lead you, Oliver. Just tug sharply on the leash to get him to walk beside you. If you let him get away with it, he'll try to do it every time he's taken for a walk."

Oliver listened intently and followed Finn's instructions. Within a matter of minutes, he'd gotten Boomer under control.

"Hey, buddy. I think we need to talk," Finn said, trying to make his voice sound casual.

Oliver looked up at him with big eyes. "Did I do something wrong?"

"No, little man. I think I might have done something wrong. Yesterday when we had our flying adventure you were upset about your mom going out on a date."

"It's okay, Finn. It doesn't matter. She went anyway," Oliver said with a shrug. Finn's lips twitched.

"You said something that surprised me. About wanting me to be your father."

"It's true. I do."

Finn felt as if his heart might crack wide-open. Oliver's little voice was filled with sincerity. It was amazing, Finn realized, how open and honest kids were. They laid it all out there, risking getting their hearts broken and their hopes dashed. Oliver's wide-open heart gutted Finn.

Finn reached out and clasped Oliver by the shoulder. "Oliver, that's the biggest and best compliment anyone has ever bestowed on me." He smiled at Oliver. "Life isn't as simple as we'd like it to be. Matter-of-fact, it's pretty complicated."

Oliver looked down and focused on Boomer. "So you don't want to be my dad, huh? I kind of figured."

"Hey, that's not it. I imagine being your dad would be the most awesome thing in the world."

Oliver looked at him, tears shimmering in his eyes. "Really?"

"Yes, really. But you can't just snap your fingers and pick a dad, Oliver. Your mom has a say in who your father's going to be. That's the way it works. And it's best when the mother and father are in love," Finn said, fighting past a lump in his throat. "Because a home filled with love is the best home of all."

"My dad used to say all the time that I was the best thing he'd ever done," Oliver said. He swiped away tears from his cheeks. "Sometimes I miss him so much it feels like I'm going to burst. I've been thinking if I found a new dad it wouldn't hurt as much."

"I know what it feels like to lose a parent. When my

mom died it felt like the sun had been extinguished. For a long time, it seemed as if there was nothing good anywhere in this world."

Oliver nodded. "I felt the same way. It's been better since we moved here. I don't cry myself to sleep every night like I used to."

"Oliver, when we lose someone special there's an ache on our souls. It lessens over time but it never completely goes away. If you find a dad here in Love, that will be terrific. But it won't necessarily stop you from feeling sad about your dad."

"I guess you're right," Oliver said. "My mom cries sometimes. She says it's like a rushing river when you lose someone."

"Your mom is one smart woman," Finn said with a nod of his head. Maggie was right. Grief was like a rushing river. It hit you when least expected. It could be wild and out of control. Unpredictable.

"I want to make sure you understand this one huge thing. You deserve an outstanding father because you're an incredible, loving, amazing boy. And if I had to guess, I'd say you're going to get your wish one of these days. Be patient."

"It's okay if you can't be my dad, Finn. 'Cause you're already my best friend."

Finn cleared his throat. Words eluded him. He wanted to grab Oliver and hug him for all he was worth. *His best friend.* Finn would accept that title with honor. And if he wasn't so afraid of messing up Oliver's life, Finn would fight to earn the title of father.

Chapter Ten

As soon as Maggie and Oliver arrived at the winter carnival on the town square, it felt to Maggie as if the entire town of Love embraced her. People approached her and introduced themselves, extending condolences to her about Uncle Tobias and welcoming her to town. Many expressed their enthusiasm about the grand opening of Keepsakes. It was nice to see all of the Prescott brothers—Cameron, Liam and Boone—happily settled down with their other halves. Their younger sister, Honor, who had been a toddler when Maggie had last seen her, was now a lovely young woman.

"Maggie Richards!" Maggie spun around at the sound of her name being called.

Dwight Lewis hadn't changed in two decades. He looked remarkably similar to the bespectacled, bow tie–wearing boy who had preferred math equations to chasing frogs in the Nottingham Woods. Seeing him after all these years served as a blast from the past.

"Dwight!" Maggie greeted him. He pulled her into

a friendly hug. Maggie felt a groundswell of emotion. Even though she and Finn had joked about Dwight the other day, it felt wonderful to see another childhood friend. She felt a little bad about hiding from him, although Keepsakes hadn't been ready for prying eyes.

A thin, dark-haired woman stood beside him. Dwight reached for the woman's hand and laced it with his own. "Maggie, I'd like to introduce you to Marta Svenson, my fiancée. Marta, this is my childhood pal Maggie Richards. She's come back to Love after a long absence."

Dwight was beaming with happiness. It bounced off him in waves. Maggie felt overjoyed for him and Marta. Finding love was truly a wonderful thing.

It felt nice to be in the thick of things. For too long she had burrowed herself in the shop and neglected making the acquaintances of the townsfolk. Many remembered her from her childhood visits to town. It was very humbling. And heartwarming.

Seeing the square lit up with holiday lights was a spectacular experience. Oliver's eyes were lit up with joy. As far as the eye could see were Christmas lights— colored lights, white lights, sparkling lights. They extended throughout the downtown area. Jarvis Street was lit up in spectacular fashion. It was a breathtaking sight to behold. The Free Library of Love was decked out in red and green flashing lights.

So far she hadn't seen Finn. Oliver kept asking for him over and over again as they explored the lights and ice sculptures. He had been looking forward to spending time with Finn this evening. As a diversion she sent him to play with Aidan and a few children from school. Maggie stood and watched from a distance as Oliver raced around the square with absolute abandon. Her chest tightened with pride. He was acclimating nicely to this wonderful town. A casual observer would never have known he was a newcomer to Love.

All of a sudden Maggie spotted a flash of red and a rugged frame. It was Finn! He had walked up to Oliver and lifted him up from behind. Finn was spinning him around in circles. Maggie didn't need to see Oliver's expression. She knew he was grinning from ear to ear.

"They're so sweet together." Ruby walked up beside her and jutted her chin in the direction of Finn and Oliver.

"They really are," Maggie acknowledged. "Oliver is Finn's biggest fan. And Finn is so attentive and caring. He's been a wonderful friend for both of us."

"Are the two of you…circling around each other?" Ruby's brown eyes were twinkling with interest.

"Not at all. We're just friends." She quirked her mouth. "Finn isn't looking for an instant family. Or a wife. And I need stability for Oliver." She made a face. "I actually caved and went out on a date with Hank Jeffries."

"How was it? Any sparks?" Ruby asked, curiosity glinting in her eyes. "I know you said you're not really looking for romance."

Maggie shook her head. "Hank is a nice man and dinner was delicious, but I can't really see anything developing between us. As much as Oliver has let it be known he wants a father, I'm not interested in a romantic relationship. I'm still dealing with my husband's death. Romance is the last thing on my list."

"Of course you're still grieving his loss, Maggie. Losing a spouse is one of the most traumatic life events a person can go through. Not to mention you've moved all the way to an Alaskan fishing village far away from home. You have to give yourself time." Ruby patted her on the shoulder. "But, somewhere down the road you might be ready to open up your heart to the possibilities. Speaking as a mother, your life doesn't begin and end as a mom. You need to be happy too."

Maggie said. "That's very true. Everyone deserves to be content in their lives."

Happiness. For so long Maggie hadn't even considered her own joy. Back in Massachusetts she'd been so miserable in the aftermath of Sam's death. And if she was being honest with herself, her marriage had been rocky for quite some time prior to the tragic loss of her husband. Sam Daviano had put her through the ringer during their marriage. Arrests for petty crimes. Chronic unemployment. Verbal abuse. In the aftermath of his death she had even changed Oliver's last name to Richards in order to avoid the stigma associated with his father. In the end, there had been nothing left for them in Boston.

Moving to Alaska had transformed Maggie's life. Day by day, she was building a life for herself and Oliver. There were moments of pure happiness where she knew they were both healing. The residents of Love made Maggie feel as if she'd landed right where God intended her to be.

And it had everything to do with being in this small fishing village, her friendship with Finn and the remarkable people who were helping her find peace in Love.

After parting ways with Oliver, Finn headed over to the concession stand. All of the proceeds from the winter carnival event were going to a homeless shelter in Homer. He surveyed the goodies. Sugar cookies. Cupcakes decorated with frosting reindeers. *Bûche de Noël* cake. He had to admit his Christmas cookies looked delectable. At least half of them had already sold. He didn't have much of a sweet tooth, but these items looked scrumptious. He imagined Oliver would get a kick out of the whimsical baked goods.

Finn still hadn't come face-to-face with Maggie, although he'd spotted her from a distance. He was deliberately keeping away in case Hank and Maggie had come here together this evening. Although he liked to think he was taking the high road, it still irritated him that Maggie and Hank could potentially be the next It couple in town. He shook the feeling off, stuffing it down to a place where he wouldn't have to examine his emotions.

"Your cookies look good. I'd recognize them anywhere." Declan's voice heralded his arrival before Finn saw him.

"Thanks. Why aren't you out there at the dogsledding track?" Finn asked, jutting his chin toward the dogsled area. Declan had always been a huge fan of the sport.

"Annie was feeling a bit tuckered out, so I was keeping her company. I didn't want her to run the risk of falling off the sled. Liam says fatigue is normal at this stage of her pregnancy, so I'm trying not to worry."

"Makes sense. Liam wouldn't steer you wrong," Finn said in a reassuring voice. He could see the worried expression etched on Declan's face. To say Annie was Declan's world was an understatement. "Speaking of Annie, where is your better half?" Finn asked, looking around the area for his sister-in-law.

"She's somewhere talking to Jasper about the town council vote on library funds. At which point I recused myself from the conversation," Declan said in a dry voice.

Finn chuckled. Knowing Annie, she was reading the town mayor the riot act. He almost wished he could witness it. Not many people could go head-to-head with Jasper.

Just then Finn caught sight of Maggie. She was wearing a puffy white coat with matching ski pants. On her head was a jaunty pink hat that was tilted to the side. Her cheeks were rosy and the tip of her nose was pink. He couldn't help smiling.

"Go on over, Finn. You know you want to talk to her," Declan said, jabbing him in the side.

He scowled at his brother. "Declan, will you give it a rest? Stop meddling. You're acting like you're twelve years old."

Declan held up his hands. "All right. I won't say another word." He held up his hand. "Scout's honor."

Finn couldn't help but chuckle. Declan always managed to make him laugh. "You were never a Boy Scout. Not even close."

Declan snorted. "Neither were you!" Finn smiled, enjoying the familiar rhythms of his relationship with his brother. He prayed they would continue to grow and strengthen as siblings.

"Finn! Finn!" Oliver was calling to him from across the way. Finn waved at him, then beckoned him over. The boy grabbed Maggie by the hand and began pulling her toward Finn and Declan.

"I'm going to go find my lady," Declan said, crossing paths with Maggie and Oliver and exchanging pleasantries as they passed by. Declan turned back toward Finn and winked at him in an exaggerated manner.

"I've been looking for you everywhere," Oliver said as soon as he reached Finn's side. "I wanted to show you the dragon ice sculpture."

"You should have known I'd be over here by the snacks," Finn said in a teasing voice. He rubbed his stomach. "They've got some mouthwatering treats, including my very own gingerbread cookies."

Oliver rubbed his mittened hands together. "Ooh. I love gingerbread."

"Hi, Finn. How are you?" Maggie greeted him with a warm smile.

"I'm good. Are you having fun?" he asked.

She nodded her head. "This is a wonderful holiday event. Everyone is so down-to-earth and welcoming. They really know how to make a person feel at home."

"Are you here alone? Or…did Hank come with you?" Finn blurted out the question before he could reel himself in.

Maggie wrinkled her nose. "No, I didn't come with Hank tonight. Oliver and I came together."

"No?" he asked, as a feeling of relief swept over him. Thoughts of Hank being with Maggie had been gnawing at him. Suddenly, Finn felt on top of the world.

"Did you guys get a dogsled ride?"

Maggie bit her lip. "No. I haven't ridden on one since I was a kid."

"So what? It's like riding a bike. You'll be fine."

Maggie shook her head vehemently. "Nope. It's not going to happen. I don't need a broken ankle or a bruised hip if I fall off. Thank you very much. Those dogs go so fast."

"Come on, Mags. I'll ride with you and Oliver. I'll even hold your hand and keep you from falling off if that's what's worrying you." The image of them riding together made Finn feel like a kid all over again.

Maggie began to giggle. Finn loved seeing the way her eyes crinkled and the sides of her mouth twitched. He looked at Oliver, who was watching him watch Maggie. He had a glint in his eye and Finn had the strangest feeling wheels were turning in his six-year-old mind.

"Mom said she'll ride the dogsled," Oliver piped up. He was grinning from ear to ear.

Maggie held up her hand. "I said maybe. It wasn't a promise, Oliver."

"But, Mom, they're only here for the winter carnival." Oliver's face fell. "They came all the way from Nome."

"Oliver, I didn't buy any tickets. And the line is really long," Maggie said, pointing toward the team of huskies.

Finn didn't know if this was becoming a habit, but he

found himself wanting to make everything right with Oliver's world. The kid had him wrapped around his little finger.

"Well, I just happen to have some pull with the person who brought the huskies to town." He turned to Maggie as Oliver began hooting and hollering.

"How about it, Maggie? Let's ride the dogsled for old times' sake."

Finn's invitation to take a ride on the dogsleds made Maggie feel like the ten-year-old version of herself. If she closed her eyes, she could picture them being led by the pack of huskies with the wind whipping against their faces and snow gently falling all around them. It had been pure joy.

"I have a surprise for your mother." Finn's huge grin threatened to overtake his face.

"What is it?" Oliver asked, jumping up and down with excitement.

"Why don't the two of you grab some hot chocolate? I'll be right back." Finn dashed off, leaving the two of them wondering what he was up to. Maggie walked to the concession stand with Oliver and bought two hot chocolates, as well as one of the reindeer cupcakes for Oliver. Before she knew it, Oliver had stuffed half of the cupcake in his mouth. He swigged it down with some gulps of hot chocolate. Maggie shook her head. She hoped Oliver wasn't going to be on too much of a sugar high.

Live in the moment, she reminded herself. Tonight was special and she wasn't going to ruin it by focusing too much on the sweets table. Her son was happier than she had seen him in well over a year. That in itself made Maggie feel like doing a jig.

Thank You for blessing us with this evening, Lord. For the fellowship and goodwill of this wonderful community. And thank You for bringing Finn back into my life and for allowing him to be a guiding light for Oliver. We are truly blessed.

By the time Oliver had finished the cupcake and hot chocolate, Finn was walking back toward them with Aidan at his side. He was holding a bunch of tickets in his hand. "It's official. We have tickets for the dogsled."

Oliver began cheering. "Yippee!" he yelled.

"I told you I had a little surprise," Finn said. He pulled a sled from behind his back—an old-fashioned wooden one with red trim. Although the sled was worn down, Maggie instantly recognized it.

"Are you kidding me?" Maggie asked. She raised her mittened hands to cover her mouth.

"I wouldn't kid about this," Finn said. "This sled is a classic and a cherished memory."

Maggie reached out and traced the faded letters spelling out her name. "After all these years you still have it? I can't believe it."

"It's seen better days, but it's been sitting in the attic all this time."

Oliver frowned. "What's so special about it?"

"This was your mother's sled," Finn explained to Oliver. "She used to ride like the wind down Cupid's Hill over at Deer Run Lake. I'll have to take you there sometime so you can sled with Aidan."

"That would be awesome," Aidan said in an excited voice.

Oliver's jaw dropped. "Wow. You must have been cool back then, Mom."

Maggie and Finn began to laugh. Aidan giggled.

"We sure thought we were," Maggie said. "Finn was pretty mischievous. This sled actually belonged to Declan. Finn borrowed it then wrote my name on it. You should have seen the steam coming out of Declan's ears."

"No one ever accused me of being a choirboy," Finn said in a teasing voice.

"No, they never did," Maggie said in a low voice as memories of the first time she'd ever met Finn flashed into her mind. It had been straight after church service and he'd tried to frighten her by putting a frog down the back of her shirt. Maggie had chased after him and, after giving him a piece of her mind, she'd accepted an invitation to go salamander hunting with him. It had been an auspicious beginning to a wonderful friendship.

"So, Mom. Are you going to ride on the dogsled?" Oliver asked. "Aidan and I are going to head over there."

"I don't know, Oliver. It's been a long time," she said, suddenly feeling a little anxious. She wasn't a kid anymore. What business did she have racing around and being led by a pack of huskies?

Oliver shrugged and walked away with Aidan.

"That's unacceptable, Maggie Richards," Finn said in a scolding voice as soon as Oliver was gone. "I seem to recall you're saying you wanted to be brave. Am I right? What could be braver than racing like the wind on a dogsled and showing your son how it's done?"

Maggie rolled her eyes. "You're not going to give up on this, are you?"

Finn smirked and shook his head. "Nope. Absolutely not."

With a sigh of resignation, Maggie tucked her sled behind a bush for safekeeping and turned back toward Finn. "Let's do this," she said, motioning toward the area where the huskies were gathered to take people on rides.

When they got to the dogsled track, Maggie watched as Aidan and Oliver stood together in line. Their little faces were full of excitement. Seeing their blossoming friendship reminded her of the way she and Finn had done the same dogsled run twenty years ago.

"Hold on tight!" Maggie called out as she watched the boys settle onto the dogsled with one of the mushers, then take off down the snowy path as the beautiful huskies exhibited their speed and power. She heard Olivier cry out with delight as they headed out of sight. When it was her turn to ride with Finn she held on tightly and prayed to make it back in one piece. Despite her nerves, it was an exhilarating feeling to fly across the snow-packed ground with the frosty air lashing against her cheeks. When they returned to the starting point she could hear Oliver and Aidan loudly cheering for them.

Gliding across the snow led by the team of huskies was a thrill ride for Maggie. She loved the exciting feeling of being pulled by the dogs at breakneck speed. After two rides, Maggie was chilled to the bone and done with dogsledding, although Oliver and Aidan wanted to continue to stand in line for another ride. Maggie chuckled. The boys didn't even seem to feel the cold.

"Why don't we go get something to drink to warm us up?" Finn suggested. He pointed at Oliver and Aidan. "These two will be fine. Something tells me they might go on a few more runs. I gave Oliver some extra tickets. He seems determined to use them."

"Oh, Finn, you're going to spoil him. I can't remember the last time we had so much fun," Maggie gushed. Even though her face felt slightly frozen, her teeth chattered and her wool mittens were slightly wet, Maggie wasn't about to complain. This evening had been stellar.

"This is one of my favorite town events," Finn said. "You can almost feel Christmas flowing in the air." He rubbed his hands together. "The lights are spectacular." He winked at Maggie. "I reckon they could spot us from space."

They made their way to the concession area where Finn bought two hot apple ciders and sugar cookies. Maggie didn't miss the curious glances thrown their way. She felt a moment of discomfort when she saw Hank watching them from across the way. She imagined everyone thought something romantic was brewing between her and Finn. Hazel began waving at her from behind the concession stand. She pointed toward Finn and gave Maggie a thumbs-up sign. Maggie frowned at Hazel and shook her head insistently, but Hazel continued to grin.

Maggie frowned. First Ruby. And now Hazel. She

didn't want to have to explain to everyone later on about her platonic relationship with Finn. Was she sending out signals about wanting more than friendship? How could she expect Oliver not to get confused when most of the town seemed to be questioning their status?

"Don't mind the looks and the stares," Finn instructed. "In a place called Love, the residents are always looking for the next couple. Don't let it bother you."

"I'm sure they mean well, but it's a little nerve-racking."

"I grabbed a blanket from the warming area. If we sit over there you can keep an eye on Oliver without him seeing us," Finn suggested. "Plus, we won't have to be the object of any whispers."

Maggie nodded in agreement. She was fine with Oliver dogsledding, but she didn't mind watching him from a discreet distance. And Maggie had never enjoyed being stared at. Although the townsfolk of Love weren't being mean-spirited, she had endured enough stares in Boston to last a lifetime.

As they moved toward a quiet area with a clear view of the dogsled track, Finn found a perfect spot and took a moment to lay a blanket down on the ground. They both sat and got comfortable.

"I have some hand warmers if you need them," Finn said, patting his jacket pocket.

"I'm good for now. This cup is really warming up my hands."

They each sipped their warm ciders. With a full moon set amid an onyx sky, Maggie couldn't help but admire the beautiful surroundings. She felt so tranquil and relaxed. She knew it wasn't just the winter carnival or the townsfolk or Oliver's effusive joy.

"Do you think I've changed a lot?" Maggie asked Finn. Being here tonight at the winter carnival reminded her of the last time she'd been at a holiday event here in town. It had felt like a trip down memory lane. She had been ten years old. A lifetime ago for all intents and purposes. Sometimes she wished she still had a sense of childhood wonder. Back then she hadn't been nervous at all about riding a dogsled. Over the years she'd become more of an anxious person. Pushing past those fears was the best remedy for anxiety. She was trying really hard in all areas of her life to be braver than she felt.

"Not really. Maybe a little bit. Have I?" Finn asked. He ran his hand across his jaw. "Aside from growing into a ruggedly handsome man," he said in a teasing voice, "I think I'm still me."

"At first you seemed really different," Maggie said. She smirked at him. "But once I scratched the surface, you're the same old Finn."

"Thanks. I think," he said with a low-throated chuckle.

"I meant it as a compliment. Sometimes I feel like the best parts of me ended up being chewed up by life. You remind me of a time and place when I was a better version. I wasn't so anxious or jaded. And lately I've been wondering if I passed it on to Oliver. He can be a worrywart sometimes."

"I don't believe that, Maggie. Do you know why? Because of Oliver. That kid has more heart than anyone I know, except for his mother. Where do you think that came from?"

Maggie shook her head. "I'm not sure he got that from me. I've been so afraid, Finn. Afraid of taking chances. Afraid of the sky falling in." She shrugged. "Just plain afraid. I'm ashamed to admit it, but I get really anxious sometimes worrying about things that are out of my control."

He reached out and squeezed her mittened hand. "You have nothing to be embarrassed about. Everyone has fears. We all worry. Give yourself a break, Mags. You've been through a lot. That takes a toll on a person."

"You're right. It does," Maggie said. "I don't like the feeling of things being out of my control. But the reality is, life often is unpredictable."

"I get it. When my grandfather got sick I felt as if my world had tilted on its axis." He bowed his head. "My emotions were all over the place. Fear had me in its grip. I knew there was nothing I could do to keep him in this world and it made me panic. I ran away from the pain of losing him. In the process, I cut myself off from all the people I loved and who loved me in return." Finn cleared his throat. "I didn't get to say goodbye to him. Fear cost me that moment."

She reached out and placed her hand on Finn's knee. "I'm sorry you missed saying your final farewell to him. There was so much love between the two of you. I hope you've been able to hold on to that."

"It's been easier to focus on the good memories ever since I returned. Now that I'm no longer running I can finally breathe a little easier. There's something about being back home that's been healing in a lot of ways."

Maggie looked at Finn as surprise washed over her. She felt the same way about being in Love. There was something so special about this heartwarming Alaskan town. "Honestly, I've felt different ever since I stepped off that seaplane. I feel braver than I've felt in years. And hopeful."

Finn nodded. "Hope is a wonderful thing."

They locked gazes. "I'll tell you a secret, Mags. You were my first crush," Finn admitted.

Maggie let out a squeal. "Really?"

"Yes, ma'am. I used to wonder if you were crushing on me as well." He wiggled his eyebrows at her. "So? The moment of truth has arrived. Were you?"

Maggie ducked her head down. Her cheeks felt flushed. She shouldn't be embarrassed. This was Finn. Her childhood pal. But with his soulful green eyes and rugged good looks, Maggie was having a hard time keeping him strictly in the friend zone. Adrenaline did tend to course through her veins whenever he was in her orbit. As children, her feelings for Finn had been strictly platonic.

"To be honest, no, Finn. It wasn't until much later that I developed romantic feelings for anyone. I think I was sixteen. A late bloomer, I suppose. I think being around my mother made me wary of developing feelings for anyone. After all, she chased anything with a pulse. It didn't make for a very stable childhood." She met Finn's gaze head-on. "But I'll tell you one thing, Finn O'Rourke. I thought you were the best thing since sliced bread. You were the most impressive, courageous and wonderful boy I'd ever met. You showed me how to run freely and embrace everything the world has to offer. And you didn't treat me differently because I was a girl. You taught me not to be so fearful. And you changed me for the better. Every time I left Love I felt stronger and more confident. I owe you a debt of gratitude for that."

Finn placed his hand over his heart. "That means the world to me. I thought about you long after you left Love for the last time. I kept hoping you'd come back. But you never did."

"I thought we would come back too. When we left here that last time I never knew it would be twenty years before I came back to Love." She quirked her mouth. "My mother fought with Uncle Tobias over her lifestyle. He wanted us to stay in Love so I could have a stable upbringing." She shook her head as bitter memories rose to the surface. "She was always chasing the next best husband. So instead of coming back here we moved to Arizona, then California and New Mexico before heading to New England."

Finn let out a low whistle. "That's a lot of moving around."

Maggie nodded. "It was rough. That's why I want Oliver to stay rooted in one place. Stability is important for children."

"Is your mom still around?" Finn asked.

"Yeah, she's living out in Las Vegas with a new husband. We're not close. There's no getting around it. My childhood was a train wreck."

"That's too bad," Finn said. "I guess both of us were going through a lot of dysfunction at the same time."

She squeezed his hand tightly. "I feel bad complaining when you lost so much."

Finn looked at her. A bittersweet expression was etched on his face. "Pain is pain, Maggie. It's hard to compare battle wounds. And you don't have to feel bad about anything. It's all right to feel whatever you're feeling."

"On a good day my feelings are all over the place," Maggie admitted.

"That's what I admire most about you. Your ability to be open and honest. So many people have a filter. You're genuine, Mags. You always have been."

Maggie felt her cheeks flush at Finn's compliment. Their faces were so close together and Finn was gazing into her eyes with such a tender look. Maggie looked up at him, wondering if she was misinterpreting what was about to happen next. Unless she was imagining things, Maggie was fairly certain she was about to kissed by Finn O'Rourke.

Chapter Eleven

Finn looked into Maggie's eyes and knew he was mere seconds away from kissing her. He tried his best to resist, knowing he was going against every vow he'd made about getting romantically involved with Maggie. He wasn't any good for her. She deserved someone solid. A father for Oliver. A man who could pledge eternity to her. He was filled with so much fear and anxiety about hurting the people he cared about. And if he was being honest with himself, he didn't trust himself to go the distance. In so many ways, Finn didn't fit the bill of what Maggie needed or wanted.

But in this moment everything stilled and hushed between them. It was just the two of them—him and his beautiful, sweet Mags. She was radiant in every single way imaginable. He reached out and stroked the line of her jaw with his fingers. She was so incredibly lovely. With her creamy skin and vivid eyes, Maggie was a knockout. Those same eyes were looking at him now with a mixture of anticipation and wonder.

"Maggie, I'm not sure I have the right to kiss you, but if I'm being completely honest with you, there's nothing I'd rather do at this moment." His voice sounded raspy to his own ears. He wanted this more than he'd wanted anything in his entire life. That very thought worried him, but he stuffed the feeling down and focused on this interlude between him and Maggie. There was a lot to be said about living in the moment.

"I—I haven't been kissed in a long time, but I'd very much like for you to kiss me." Her voice was soft yet steady. It rang out with truth.

The raw honesty in Maggie's words propelled Finn forward. He lowered his head, letting out a sigh as his lips touched Maggie's. He placed his lips over hers in a tender, soaring kiss. She smelled like a mixture of the great outdoors and a light vanilla scent.

For Finn, this kiss was everything. It was friendship and romance and attraction. It was the ties binding the two of them together for decades. It represented new beginnings.

As the kiss ended, Finn knew with a deep certainty all kisses weren't created equal. He had kissed enough women in his life to realize this was special. Powerful. Spectacular. Seconds ticked by during which their foreheads touched and neither said a word. He could hear the low sound of his breathing and see the rapid rise and fall of her chest. At the same time, he knew he'd just made a colossal mistake.

"Finn, what does this mean?" Maggie asked, her voice full of uncertainty. "For us? I don't want to lose our friendship or put a strain on it."

"I don't know, but I do know I'm at my best when I'm with you, Maggie. I feel more like me than I ever do with anyone else," Finn admitted. He didn't know exactly how to put into words the way he was feeling. But he knew it felt right when Maggie was in his arms. She was rapidly becoming his best friend all over again. Finn cared so very much about her well-being. As a result, he couldn't stuff down the niggling feelings of doubt roaring through him. He wanted to try with Maggie. He yearned to be the man who could make her and Oliver happy, but he worried about hurting both of them. If he harmed either one of them, he would never forgive himself.

Finn opened his mouth to tell Maggie his truth. Kissing her had been a mistake. It had been a selfish move on his part since he knew it couldn't go anywhere. Maggie wasn't the type of woman a man should trifle with.

"Hey, Mom! There you are!" Oliver's chirpy voice interrupted them as he suddenly appeared in front of them. His cheeks were flushed with cold and his snow pants were damp. "I was looking for you everywhere."

Maggie grinned at her son. "I think it's time we headed home, Oliver. Your eyes are getting a little droopy and your cheeks are as red as a berry." Finn jumped up and lent a hand to Maggie, pulling her to her feet. For a moment their eyes locked. Something crackled in the air between them.

"C'mon," Oliver said, his voice full of fatigue. "I want to say goodbye to Aidan."

As they walked back toward the concession stand where the residents were gathered, Finn's mind was full of regrets. Even though kissing Maggie had been a moment of pure tenderness and connection, Finn couldn't allow himself to believe in a happy ending.

Sharing this precious time with Maggie hadn't changed a single thing. He still felt unworthy of a happily-ever-after.

Maggie had been fretting about the kiss she'd shared with Finn ever since the night of the winter carnival. She'd tried not to focus on it, but it felt like the elephant in the room whenever she and Finn were in the same area. She didn't know if she was imagining it or not, but things felt slightly awkward. Maggie wasn't used to kissing a man she wasn't attached to romantically. Although the past few days had been filled with completing the final days of setup for Keepsakes, she was preoccupied by her conversation with Finn the other night. He had praised her for being open and honest. Forthright. It bothered her to think she was keeping secrets from him, especially when he had been so transparent about his mother's accidental death.

Maggie couldn't hold off any longer. She wanted to tell Finn the truth about the circumstances of Sam's death. At this point, it felt like a lie to withhold such information. It was weighing her down like an anchor. Finn was her best friend here in town. It would feel therapeutic to get it off her chest.

Lord, please help me get the words right. I don't want Finn to think I've lied to him about Sam. And I pray he'll understand why I kept silent. I know Finn's heart—he's a strong, good man.

Maggie cooked that evening for her, Finn and Oliver. It was her specialty—spaghetti Bolognese with garlic bread and salad. Oliver had put both her and Finn on the spot by begging Finn to come for dinner. Maggie didn't mind since she'd been searching for an opportunity to have a private conversation with Finn. After tucking her son into bed, she stood at the sink and washed the dinner dishes, with Finn drying and putting them back on the shelves.

"Everything okay?" Finn asked. "You seem a bit preoccupied. I hope you're not worrying about the grand opening. We're in great shape."

Maggie shook her head. "It's not the shop." She bit her lip. "You've been so honest with me about your mother's death. It's made me feel a little bit ashamed."

Finn raised an eyebrow. "Ashamed? Of what?"

"I haven't been completely straightforward about my husband's death."

Finn frowned. His handsome features were creased in confusion. "What do you mean?"

Maggie took a deep breath. "He wasn't the victim of a store robbery. The truth is he was holding it up for money." Her voice quivered. "The store owner shot and killed him in self-defense."

Finn's jaw dropped. He stumbled for something to say in response to Maggie's confession. His mind whirled with the reality of her situation. Not only was she a widowed single mother, but she had been traumatized by the extreme circumstances of her husband's death. Her husband had single-handedly destroyed their family with his actions.

Finn's heart began to pound like crazy in his chest.

Maggie wiped away a tear. "Sam lived a double life. He had gotten into trouble with the law from time to time over the years, but mostly for small things." She let out a harsh-sounding laugh. "Not that it didn't matter, but I had no idea he was robbing stores. He grew up in really abusive foster homes, so I think I made a lot of excuses for him. I can honestly say I didn't see it coming."

"When the police came to my door that night I was in utter shock. I kept thinking Sam was the victim of the robbery because it was the only thing I could fathom. Then it became agonizingly clear he was a very troubled man. One I'd been married to for seven years."

Finn's heart was breaking for her and Oliver. It must have rocked their world to its core to have been blindsided in such a shocking way. "Maggie, I'm so sorry you went through all of that. It must have been agonizing."

"We went through a lot in the aftermath." Maggie ducked her head. "People weren't very nice."

Finn gritted his teeth. "What did they do?"

"I lost my job. We got phone calls and harassing letters. Our landlord kicked us out. Even our church community turned their backs on us. Most of the parents of Oliver's friends wouldn't allow their children to have playdates with him. We lost everything all at once."

Her voice faltered. "What I'll never understand is why people were so cruel to us. Why they blamed us. We were victims too. We lost our lives." Maggie's voice was laced with agony.

"It makes no sense as to why people choose to act in such a mean-spirited way. It's the very opposite of the way we're supposed to treat each other. I'll never understand it, but I do know good people outweigh the bad in this world." Finn deeply believed it. His faith taught him to do unto others and love one another.

"You're right, Finn. That's a good way to look at things," Maggie said with a nod.

There was no doubt as to how much she and Oliver had suffered due to her ex-husband. Maggie had been terribly wounded by her husband's actions and subsequent death. His heart bled for Maggie and Oliver. To suffer the condemnation of one's community after such a tragedy was shocking. He stuffed down a desire to head to Boston and deal with those small-minded people who had hurt Maggie. He'd like to give them a piece of his mind and a dose of their own medicine.

He hated cruelty, especially toward a defenseless and grief-stricken mother and child. It was the very opposite of the way he wanted to live his life.

"Why were you afraid to come clean about it here in Love?" he asked, hating how Maggie had been so consumed with worry about her past. Finn prayed she would put all of it to rest so she could focus on her future.

"Because of all the judgment we endured. Coming here was about making a fresh start. I couldn't risk losing the goodwill of the people here before we even stepped into town."

"That would never happen," Finn said, wanting Maggie to understand this town was different. It was far from perfect, but he knew without a shadow of a doubt the townsfolk would extend Maggie grace and brotherly love.

"I know that now, but at the time I didn't. I could take it for me, but not for Oliver. He's just a child. And God knows he's innocent in all of this. Children shouldn't suffer the sins of the father." Her voice broke and she began to sob.

Finn placed an arm around Maggie and pulled her close. "He won't, Maggie. Oliver is happy and thriving here in Love. You did the very best thing you could for him. You stepped out on a limb of faith and came back to Alaska. You seized an opportunity to make a better life for yourself and Oliver. Those are commendable things."

A hint of a smile appeared on her face. "Thank you for saying so, Finn. I'm very grateful to be here in Alaska. I just felt a little funny about not coming clean with you. You've been so open and honest with me."

"Maggie, you don't owe the town or me an explanation of your past. If you wish to share that information, then so be it."

"I'm grateful for your listening ears, Finn. And for accepting me, warts and all."

As Finn drove home, his thoughts swirled with thoughts of Maggie and all she'd endured because of her ex-husband. It made his chest tighten painfully. And he knew with a sinking feeling in his gut that the information he'd learned tonight confirmed everything he felt about the possibility of building something with Maggie. It just wasn't possible.

There was no way he could risk subjecting Maggie

to any more hurt. He didn't trust himself not to mess everything up. What if he did something to hurt them? What if he destroyed them the same way he had torn apart his own family? What if he did worse damage than Sam had done?

How could he risk it? Maggie and Oliver had already been through so much. Way more than he had ever imagined or could even bear to think about. Finn felt sick to his stomach. By kissing Maggie, he may have led her to believe a relationship was possible between them when he knew it wasn't. He should have just left well enough alone and let Maggie develop something with Hank. A man like Hank wouldn't let Maggie down in the clutch. With one impulsive kiss he had complicated things. His timing couldn't have been worse. They were on the cusp of the grand opening for Keepsakes. His future as a co-owner of O'Rourke Charters was just within reach. It was the one dream he'd allowed himself to hold on to through the years.

Any hopes of being with Maggie and Oliver weren't realistic. One way or another, he feared he was going to hurt them. And the very thought of doing so made him feel like the worst person in the world.

Maggie felt as excited as she had always felt as a kid on Christmas morning. She was going caroling with her choir group and Finn had been invited to come along with them. The group was in dire need of altos. Maggie had to laugh. Although Finn loved to sing, he tended to sing off-key. It didn't matter, she thought. Caroling was about spreading Christmas cheer and goodwill. It was all about heart. Finn had plenty of it. And he sang with unbridled enthusiasm.

At seven o'clock sharp the carolers met on the town green. They were all dressed in old-fashioned burgundy cloaks and the women wore fur hand muffs. Snow was gently falling and there was a frost in the air.

"Where's Finn?" Oliver asked, looking around him.

Maggie frowned. Finn should have been here by now. "I don't know, love. Maybe he's going to join us or something came up with O'Rourke Charters." She made a face at Oliver. "You know he wouldn't miss this unless it was something important."

Maggie checked her phone. There were no messages from Finn. She'd been with him a few hours earlier at the shop. He'd been a little quiet, but when she had reminded him about the caroling event, he'd been on board with it. Where could he be?

They went caroling door-to-door, singing Christmas hymns and spreading the joy of the season as they walked around town. Despite her disappointment about Finn, Maggie had a fantastic time. It was a great opportunity to bond with her fellow choral singers and the residents of Love. Having Oliver by her side had provided a good opportunity to show her son the real heart of Love, Alaska.

As the event ended, a large number of the carolers headed over to the Moose Café. Much to Oliver's delight, Maggie decided to join the group. Once they entered, Maggie immediately spotted Finn. While Oliver was distracted by a few of his school friends, Maggie made a beeline over to him.

"Finn! What happened to you? We were expecting you to go caroling with us."

Finn raked his hand through his hair. He seemed to be looking everywhere but in her direction. "Hey, Maggie. I'm sorry. I had to do some paperwork for O'Rourke Charters. There's lots to do before I become Declan's partner."

"We had a good time," Maggie said, not asking Finn why he hadn't bothered to call her.

"That's good," he said in a clipped tone.

"Something's wrong," Maggie said. "What is it?" She knew Finn like the back of her hand. The expression on his face seemed distant. Something was off.

"Can we go outside for a minute?" Finn asked, his features creased with worry.

"Of course," Maggie said, following after Finn as he took the lead and headed outside.

With snowflakes swirling all around them, Finn began to speak.

"I don't want to hurt you, Maggie."

"W-what are you talking about?" she asked. Her mouth suddenly felt as dry as sandpaper.

"Us. That kiss we shared at the winter carnival. It should never have happened." He tapped his fingers against his chest. "It was all my fault for allowing it to happen. We could ruin a really good friendship. For me, it's not a risk I want to take."

Maggie felt a bit stunned. All she could do was nod. She had been hoping their kiss meant Finn had changed his mind about being in a relationship. That, combined with his clear affection for Oliver, had allowed her to have hope.

Stupid, stupid, she chided herself. Finn hadn't made her any promises. In this instance, a kiss had just been a kiss. Maggie didn't dare allow Finn to see her disappointment. Or her heartbreak.

"I understand," she murmured. Heat burned her cheeks. She'd been so foolish to believe Finn wanted something lasting with her. Hadn't he told her over and over again he wasn't interested in relationships? How could she have been so naive?

"We want different things," Finn continued. "At some point down the road you're going to want a father for Oliver. Who knows? It could be months from now or years. And I can't blame you. He deserves one after everything he's been through. And not just anyone. A great one. That can't be me. I'm not—" He fumbled with his words and his voice trailed off.

Hurt flared through her. Sharing a kiss with Finn had felt like coming home. Why was it so easy for him to push her away? Oliver's face flashed before her eyes. The way he felt about Finn was epic. He thought Finn was better and stronger than any superhero. His little heart was vulnerable. Finn was right. She couldn't risk her son being burned. She knew he wouldn't do it on purpose, but the fallout would still be the same. It was far better to end things before they even got started. She felt grateful Oliver hadn't gotten his hopes up and thankful she hadn't allowed Oliver to see how she felt about Finn. When it came to Finn, her son wore his heart on his sleeve.

"You're right. We got a little carried away with the kiss. The bottom line is I need to focus on my future. Oliver's future. My goals haven't changed. My son needs stability, and perhaps down the line a father. As you said, that can't be you."

She saw something flicker in the depths of Finn's green eyes. It looked a little bit like hurt, but she had to be mistaken. After all, Finn himself kept making the same point. He wasn't built for the long haul.

"I'm sorry to be so blunt, Maggie. I know it might sound trite, but I never in a million years want to hurt you. Or Oliver."

As if through a fog, Maggie heard Finn say goodnight before he turned on his heel and walked off into the Alaskan evening. She steeled herself against the painful feelings ricocheting through her. She blinked away the tears and steadied herself to go back inside the Moose Café.

Eyes on the prize. Finn was Alaskan eye candy, but he wasn't the marrying kind. Or the settling-down kind. He could make her laugh like nobody's business, but he didn't want to assume the role and responsibilities of a husband and father. If nothing else, Sam had taught her to doubt love everlasting. She had promised herself a long time ago that she wasn't going to allow a man into her life. Been there, done that. Her goal had been to create a stable life for Oliver. He was her world. But then Finn had crept his way into her heart.

He'd given it to her straight. Finn didn't want entanglements. Maggie was trying to be brave, but tears burned her eyes as his words washed over her. *We want different things.* He hadn't meant to be cruel. It was just the way things were. For a little while she had forgotten her own resolve to not allow her head to rule her heart. With a few little words Finn had reminded her that she didn't need a man in her life. God had given her the best gift of all by allowing her to be a mother. She didn't need any more than that in this life. Oliver was enough!

Maggie headed back inside, plastering a smile on her face so she didn't upset Oliver. He was sitting at a table acting like the life of the party with his school friends. She might be nursing a bruised heart, but at least her son was happy. She took deep little breaths and counted to ten before joining some of her friends at a nearby table. Maggie had no intention of letting anyone see her wounds.

Life had taught Maggie well. Finn might have hurt her, but she was used to love making a fool out of her. All she could do now was hold her head up high and carry on. Not just for herself, but for Oliver as well.

Chapter Twelve

Finn couldn't remember a time when he had felt so poorly. He'd left Keepsakes early today, not wanting either Maggie or Oliver to catch whatever was ailing him. His body ached and he felt feverish. He was fairly certain he was coming down with something. Maybe the flu. Or some random stomach bug. He let out a groan, wishing he could be taken out of his misery.

A part of him knew he wasn't really sick. Or at least he wasn't ill with a virus. He was aching from the reality of his situation with Maggie. For one brief moment he'd nurtured a hope about being the type of guy who could be in a normal relationship. Maggie had inspired him to feel that way. He had clung to her goodness as a way of convincing himself it was possible. Then everything had blown up in his face. Reality had come crashing down on him. It was one thing to tell yourself you weren't worthy of a loving relationship and quite another to deal with the impact of it.

Although Maggie had tried to hide it, Finn knew he'd

hurt her. And it pained him to realize he'd wounded a person he deeply cared about. Maggie didn't deserve it.

The door to his house crashed open. Finn jumped up from his couch at the jarring sound. Break-ins were unheard-of in Love. He hoped a tree branch hadn't fallen on his home.

Declan came charging toward him, his striking features etched in anger.

"What do you think you're doing?" he barked. "Why did you give up on you and Maggie? According to Hazel, you stopped things before they even got started."

Finn let out a groan. "Excuse you. You can't just come barging in to my house."

"Gimme a break, Finn. Stop trying to divert my attention. I saw the two of you at the winter carnival. It was obvious there were feelings brewing between you. You looked like a couple. Why did you bail on Maggie?"

Finn let out a groan. "I didn't bail on anyone. Not that it's any of your business, but things between Maggie and me got complicated. We're better off as friends. I'm actually doing her a favor."

Declan let out a snort. "Women are complicated, Finn. It's not rocket science."

"I'm not cut out for relationships. There! Are you happy now?"

"You love her, Finn. It's written all over your face. You show it every time you glance in her direction. Ever since Maggie's been back in Love I've seen a different side of you. One I thought was gone forever. You're happier. Your soul is lighter. You laugh more. That's because of her." Tears pooled in Declan's eyes.

"I know how much it hurt you when Mom died. It was agonizing. You've always tried to hide your hurts, but I saw your pain. You haven't been the same since then."

"What do you want me to say, Declan?" He let out a groan. "Yes, I love her. But I'm not cut out—" Finn stopped midsentence and shook his head. The words were stuck in his throat. How could he explain himself without revealing the truth about the night their mother died? And if he did, Declan might hate him for the rest of his life. He couldn't bear the thought of losing his brother. He'd already lost so many people in his life. Losing him would gut Finn.

"Don't run away from what you're feeling for Maggie. Stay. For once in your life stick around and face things."

Finn shrugged. "Who says I'm running? Maybe I'm just walking away."

"From the woman you love? Why would you do that?" Declan asked.

"Because I don't deserve her or Oliver or a nice house with a white picket fence. I don't want to hurt them."

Declan winced. "Why would you say something like that? You deserve it all, Finn."

"No, I don't. Don't you get it? It was all my fault. All of it. Every loss our family endured. It was all because of me. And I'm scared to death I'm going to do something to hurt Maggie and Oliver."

"What are you talking about?" Declan asked, his voice sounding raw and wounded. Finn knew he was hurting Declan and it killed him.

Finn swiped away tears with the back of his hand. "I can't do this. Please. Just leave it alone."

"No way. You can't say something like that and then backtrack."

Finn heaved in a ragged breath. He'd avoided this conversation for two decades. Finn felt tired. He was so incredibly weary. For so long he had carried this heavy weight on his shoulders. He was close to the breaking point.

"It was me. All me. I put the bullets in the shotgun. When I was home alone I did some shooting practice in the backyard even though I knew we weren't supposed to touch the shotgun without adult supervision. I replaced the gun right where I'd found it, but I didn't empty the shells." Finn couldn't bear to look at his brother. He didn't want to see the look of disgust on his face.

Declan let out a blast of air. "And you've been carrying this around on your shoulders for twenty years? Blaming yourself?"

"How could I not? I knew what I'd done, but I didn't tell anyone. And Dad took the blame for it. He took off and stayed gone. He even served a prison sentence after running on the wrong side of the law. If you ask me, Gramps died from a broken heart. He couldn't take all of those losses."

Declan met his gaze head-on. "That's nonsense. He died of emphysema. He'd been dealing with it for years."

"The facts don't lie. I was the one who put the bullets in the rifle. That afternoon I was home alone...ten years old and eager to try something I knew was forbidden. We were taught to always empty the shotgun. I didn't do that."

"And so what if you did? You were ten years old, Finn. A child! I was eight. It could easily have been me who played around with the shotgun."

Finn shook his head. A part of him knew Declan was right, but another part of him still couldn't let himself off the hook.

"But it wasn't you who did it! It was me!" Finn exploded.

Declan shook his head. "Finn, you've got to find a way to put this to rest once and for all. You're giving up your future! I'm not going to let you do this to yourself. Do you hear me? I won't allow you to sabotage your happiness."

Finn watched as Declan stormed away from him and out of his house. He loved his brother for trying to lift him up, but there was still so much resting on his heart. It felt as if someone had placed a heavy anchor on his chest. Try as he might, Finn still didn't think he was worthy of being with a woman like Maggie.

Chapter Thirteen

A feeling of euphoria seized Maggie as she stood outside Keepsakes and looked up at the beautiful sign. A few days ago Finn had painted it a brilliant red against a backdrop of white. "I hope we've made you proud, Uncle Tobias," Maggie murmured as she scanned the display windows. Everything looked so festive and beautiful.

After feeling down in the dumps for several days about Finn, Maggie had convinced herself to snap out of it. As Oliver's mother, she couldn't allow herself to feel disheartened for too long. And she certainly wasn't going to allow Oliver to see her mope around like a wounded bird. She was going to keep her chin up and keep moving forward. If there was any awkwardness between her and Finn, Oliver would be the one to suffer for it. She was determined to treat Finn with nothing but kindness and friendship.

When she walked back inside the shop, Finn and Oliver were playing a game of checkers. She had to smile at the sight of them. They were strong competitors. Neither one wanted to lose the match to the other. Despite what had gone down between her and Finn, she didn't want anything to change for Oliver. Finn was still a very good man. So it was best to stuff down her heartache and act like a grown-up.

Maggie looked at her watch. "We're half an hour away from launch."

Finn said something in a low voice to Oliver, who quickly began to put away the game. As Oliver tidied up, Finn walked over to the front counter and pulled something from the shelves underneath.

"I have something for you," Finn said, holding out a gaily wrapped present. His expression was sheepish.

"What? Is this for me?" Maggie asked. She felt a little bit awkward about accepting a gift from Finn after things had fizzled out between them.

Finn nodded and pushed the gift toward her. "Today's a big day. I'm happy for you, Maggie. It's been a pleasure working side by side with you to get the shop up and running. Tobias would be over the moon."

"Should I open it now?" she asked.

"Go for it," Finn said with a grin.

Maggie began unwrapping the gift, marveling at Finn's mastery of gift wrapping. Once she'd ripped away the paper, Maggie took off the top from the square box. The moment she laid eyes on the rounded glass orb, she let out a squeal.

"Oh, Finn. It's magnificent," she said. She pulled the snow globe out of the box. It was a beautiful winter scene of a skating party at a lake. She shook the snow globe, admiring the delicate flakes that floated down on the scene.

"I could tell by the way you've been admiring the snow globes here in the store they were something you really admired. I also knew it wasn't something you would buy for yourself. You always think of others first."

"Do you like it, Mom?" Oliver asked. "Finn ordered it all the way from Montana."

Maggie reached down and tweaked Oliver's nose. "I don't just like it. I love it." She met Finn's gaze. "I'll treasure it forever."

The magnitude of Finn's gift lifted Maggie up to the stratosphere. Only Finn could have figured out her life-long love of snow globes. Only Finn would have had the foresight to order her such a meaningful gift and present it to her on such a special day.

As they locked gazes, a buzz of electricity passed between them. Awareness flared in the air. She didn't know what else to say without sounding sappy. Maggie hoped she wasn't wearing her heart on her sleeve, because at this moment the love she felt for Finn threatened to burst out of her heart.

She loved him. And she couldn't imagine not loving him. Not ever. Even though she knew they couldn't be together, that knowledge did nothing to change the way she felt.

A rapping noise echoed on the door. The sound of the doorknob rattling soon followed. Maggie felt her palms moisten with nervousness. It was hard to believe the moment had arrived. Keepsakes was about to open its doors.

"I think we have our first customers," Finn drawled. He looked at his watch. "And ten minutes early no less."

"Can I open the door?" Oliver asked.

"Why don't we do it together?" Maggie suggested, placing the snow globe back in its box and tucking it away behind the counter. With a deep breath, she headed toward the door with Oliver by her side and pulled it wide open, letting out a shocked sound as she saw a line of people waiting for entry. In all of her wildest dreams, she'd never imagined so many people showing up all at once.

"Welcome to Keepsakes," Maggie said in a cheerful voice.

"Thanks for coming," Oliver chirped, a big smile plastered on his face.

Excitement hummed and pulsed in the air as the townsfolk poured through the doors of Keepsakes. A little bell jangled every time a customer walked in. The smell of peppermint wafted in the air thanks to an essential oils diffuser. They had set up a little sidebar table with eggnog and apple cider doughnuts. Every customer was given a raffle ticket for a chance to win holiday prizes. A festive vibe radiated in the shop.

Hope floated in the air around them. She prayed her efforts to bring Keepsakes back to life would make Uncle Tobias proud.

Maggie greeted each and every customer. She felt very grateful for the bustling crowd. Finn was working the register and using his charm to sell additional items to customers once they were at the counter, checking out. Despite what had transpired between them the other night, they were working together to ensure the success of the grand opening.

At Finn's suggestion, Maggie had framed a black-and-white photo of Uncle Tobias and hung it in a prominent place on the wall behind the cash register. It brought tears to her eyes to acknowledge how her uncle's kindness and generosity had affected so many lives. Maggie couldn't count the number of townsfolk who had approached her and recounted heartwarming stories about him.

With only an hour to go until the shop closed, a tall, good-looking man with gray-blue eyes walked in and a hush fell over the store. Maggie frowned as she looked around her. Hazel's jaw was practically on the floor. People were whispering and talking behind their hands. She swung her gaze to Finn. A myriad of expressions crossed his face—shock, recognition, joy.

Suddenly it hit Maggie like a ton of bricks. Although twenty years had passed since she'd last seen him, she felt fairly certain about the man's identity.

It was Colin O'Rourke, Finn's absentee father.

When Finn swung his gaze up from the cash register and spotted his father walking through the doorway, it felt as if he was having an out-of-body experience. He blinked once, then twice. He hadn't been mistaken. Colin O'Rourke had finally returned to Love, Alaska. The years had been kind to his dad. He was still a man who could turn heads by walking into a room.

Finn stepped from behind the cash register. In a few easy strides, he'd managed to intercept his father. They were the same height, Finn realized with surprise. For some reason, he always thought of his father from a child's vantage point. Taller. Stronger. Bigger.

"W-what are you doing here?" he asked in a low voice. Even though he wanted to kick his father out on his ear, he didn't want to do anything to hurt sales or ruin the grand opening of Keepsakes. Maggie had worked tirelessly to pull this off. So far, they were knocking it out of the park.

Out of nowhere, Declan appeared at his father's side. "He's here for you, Finn."

Finn felt a stab of betrayal as he locked gazes with Declan. He'd known his father was going to show up here today! And he'd allowed Finn to be blindsided. He couldn't remember ever feeling so disappointed in his brother.

Finn swung his gaze around the store. Maggie was looking at him with wide eyes. He quickly walked over to her. "I need a few minutes. Can you man the cash register?"

She bobbed her head. "Of course. Take as much time as you need."

He made his way back to his father and brother. "We can't do this here. Let's go in the back room." Without waiting for an answer, Finn strode toward the back of the store and down a small hallway. He jerked open the office door and stormed inside, followed by Colin and Declan.

He felt as if steam was coming out of his ears. This

was Maggie's grand opening. It wasn't the time or place for his father to show up out of the blue.

He scowled at his brother. "Declan! What did you do?" His question came out like a ferocious roar.

"I did what needed to be done," Declan said, his expression unapologetic. "I reached out to him."

"Son, we need to talk and it needed to be face-to-face. Man-to-man. I'm not leaving until we air things out." Colin's voice was firm, brooking no argument.

Finn let out a bitter-sounding chuckle. "Now? After all this time?"

"You're right," Colin said, shaking his head. "We're way overdue. And I apologize. To both of you. I bailed on our family. There's no excuse for the things I've done. Back then I didn't have the tools to talk openly to you about your mother's death." He winced. "Honestly, I'm not sure I do now."

Anger rose up inside Finn. "You've been gone in one way or another ever since then."

"Finn, I know there's no excuse, but my heart was broken. I'm not strong like you and Declan. And to make matters worse, it was my fault." Agony rang out in his voice. "She was my best friend. The very best of me. And when she left us, I crumbled. I lost sight of everything I held dear."

Maggie's face flashed before Finn's eyes. How would he feel if through his actions Maggie was taken from this world? He couldn't even imagine the utter devastation.

Colin frowned at him. "Declan told me you've been blaming yourself all this time," his father said.

Finn gritted his teeth. "I put the bullets in the shotgun. I went against everything I'd ever been told by you and Mom in our household." He wiped away tears with the back of his palm. He let out a groan. "Boredom set in while I was home alone. I put the bullets in and then I shot off a few rounds in the backyard. I'd lined up some cans and I wanted to see if I could hit them.

"I kept telling myself to take the bullets out so I wouldn't get in any trouble, so no one would know what I'd done. But I forgot. And then that night you were in the backyard joking around. The gun went off. We lost our whole world. Because of me."

"And you never said a word, did you? You bottled it all up inside you and let it fester." Declan's face looked tortured.

"No. How could I?" he asked in an agonized voice. "I didn't want to lose the rest of my family. I didn't want all of you to hate me."

"So instead you hated yourself." His father's words hung in the air like a grenade. Finn had never thought about it like that before. It was true. He had been struggling with feelings of poor self-worth ever since.

Finn hung his head. He didn't know what to say. How could he put into words the guilt of a child over something so monumental? How to put into words the devastation of having your father unravel and leave the family who had so desperately needed him?

His chest tightened. "We lost so much. It was a lot to bear."

"You are not responsible!" Colin said in a raised

voice. "No matter what you think you know about that night, you're wrong."

"You need to listen, Finn," Declan said. "Just listen."

"At the time I was as honest as I thought I should be about that night. You two were so young I didn't want to overwhelm you with the details. I didn't know it would be important." Colin raked his hand through his hair. "I never imagined you would blame yourself, Finn. How could I when I was the one at fault? Finn, you know how meticulous your mother was to detail. Cindy was like a bloodhound." Colin let out a sharp laugh. "Much the same way as she knew when you sneaked freshly baked peanut butter cookies from the tray, she knew you'd been playing around with the shotgun. That same day she emptied it when she realized what you'd been doing when we weren't home. We were planning to sit you down and talk to you about it, but then—" His voice trailed off.

"She died." Finn's voice sounded flat to his own ears.

"Yes, Finn, she passed. And there's not a day that goes by without my thinking of her. Mourning her. And wishing I'd never refilled the shotgun with bullets. Your mother and I had just enjoyed a wonderful night. We had dinner out at The Bay, then we came back here and drank some wine and a few beers. I was joking around with her about finally getting rid of that raccoon who kept messing with our trash." Colin's shoulders shuddered and he let out a sob. "To be honest, it all happened so fast. Like a flash. She was laughing and she lunged to take away the weapon. It was like an explosion."

For a few minutes everything was silent.

His father cleared his throat. "So you can't blame yourself, Finn. If you have to place all of this on someone's shoulders, pick mine. I'll gladly shoulder it if it brings you peace."

Finn felt as if he'd been blind for the last two decades and now he could suddenly see clearly. His father was a broken man. The death of his wife had gutted him. He'd spiraled out of control and, due to guilt and pain, abandoned his family. For many years Finn had harbored negative feelings toward the man who had given him life. But now—seeing him so shattered—it hit Finn hard. At this moment all he felt was compassion. And gratitude. It couldn't have been easy to come back after all this time and confess the truth of that night.

It was time to move past his mother's death. In Finn's opinion she had been the most loving, wonderful person in the world. Never in a million years would she have wanted her family to be eaten up by her death. She would have told them all to get a grip on themselves. Cindy O'Rourke would have hated all this angst and guilt and divisiveness.

He wanted to honor his mother. The way he was living his life wasn't doing justice to the woman who had given him life. He was throwing away every hope and dream for the future she'd worked so hard to build for him. Feeling overwhelmed, Finn bowed his head.

Lord, I need Your grace. I'm at a crossroads in my life. For so long I've been carrying all this guilt around on my shoulders. I can't carry it anymore. I'm incredibly weary. I'm not an unworthy person. I've made a lot of mistakes, but I'm still worthy of happiness. I've got to lay these burdens aside. I need to have forgiveness in my heart for my father. I've been so angry at him for something out of his control. He loved my mother more than anyone or anything. And I love Maggie. And Oliver. I need peace in my life so I can move forward and claim my future. Thank You, Lord, for allowing me to see clearly what's been in front of me all of this time.

When he opened his eyes he saw both Declan and Colin bowing their heads in prayer. He walked closer, bridging the distance between them. Without saying a word, Finn stood between them and clasped their hands in his.

"Lord, please bring us together as a family," Finn said. "Let the pain of the past be healed. Open our hearts and minds to all the possibilities stretched out before us. I ask this in Your name."

As soon as Finn stopped speaking he found himself enveloped in a hug by his father and Declan. His shoulders heaved as all of the years of painful separation and heartache melted away in the loving embrace of his family.

Chapter Fourteen

Maggie was trying not to worry about what was happening in the back room of the store. They had been sequestered for quite some time. Oliver was serving as her official greeter while she manned the cash register. There were only a few minutes left until the shop closed. They were all supposed to head over to the Moose Café, where Cameron had offered to host a small holiday party in Keepsakes's honor. Oliver was excited about having hot chocolate and s'mores and hanging out with his best buddy, Aidan.

Maggie's mind was whirling with the possibilities about the sudden appearance of Colin O'Rourke. Perhaps Colin had come back due an illness? Oh dear. She hoped it wasn't anything terrible. Or maybe he was trying to make amends at Christmas. It would be such a blessing for Finn and Declan if that was the case. The best gift of all.

When it was time to close up shop, Ruby took Oliver over to the Moose Café with her family. Maggie promised to meet up with them in a little while. She couldn't imagine what was going on in the back room. And the longer they stayed out of sight, the more she fretted. She prayed Finn was okay.

After what seemed like an eternity, Finn, Colin and Declan all emerged from the back room. Colin approached her and they exchanged pleasantries before he departed with Declan. Finn stood quietly in their wake. He was staring at the door his father and brother had just walked through.

"Finn, are you all right?" Although Maggie had accepted the fact that she and Finn didn't have a future together, she still cared about him. There was no denying it. She loved him. But she could never profess her love for him, because he didn't want it. He'd made that fact quite apparent.

"I—I think so." A dazed expression was stamped on his face.

"What was your father doing here?" Maggie asked. Finn had told her about Colin's disappearing act from his hometown. She couldn't imagine what had brought him back after all this time.

"He came to set me free," Finn said. A slow smile began to break out over his face.

Maggie wrinkled her nose. "I don't understand." She waved her hand at him. "Never mind. It's none of my business." She had promised herself to maintain a healthy emotional distance from Finn. It was the only way of protecting her heart from being smashed into pieces. She loved Finn, but she knew there was no hope of him loving her in return. Finn didn't want the same things as she did. He'd made it painfully clear to her. And if nothing else, the past had taught her to guard her heart wisely.

"Yes, it is, Maggie. Or at least I hope it is. I'm praying you care enough about me to make it your business."

Maggie's lips trembled. "I—I did care. I do care. But you made it pretty obvious you don't want me to." *Don't cry*, she reminded herself. *Be strong*.

Finn took a few steps toward her, bridging the gap between them. Maggie sucked in a deep breath at his close proximity. It was dangerous for her equilibrium to be so close to Finn. Before she could take a step backward, he reached out and placed her face between his palms.

"Maggie, I love you," he said. The expression on his face was heartfelt. Tears misted in his green eyes.

She let out a gasp. His words had almost made her knees buckle. "What did you say?" she asked, wondering if she'd misheard him. Hope soared within her heart.

He grinned at her, then dipped his head down to place a tender kiss on her lips. Being kissed by Finn was a sweet surprise. She had been under the belief such a kiss would never happen again.

"I am head over heels in love with you, Mags. I have been for a while, but I was so busy running from things that happened a long time ago I didn't feel worthy of you and Oliver. I couldn't risk causing any more pain. When you told me about Sam, it tore me up inside. I knew you'd already suffered so much."

Maggie could read between the lines about Finn's past. But she needed to hear it directly from his lips. If there was even a shot at them being together, she needed to understand so they could move forward. Not just for herself, but for Oliver as well.

Finn took a deep breath and began to tell Maggie about the night of his mother's death and the guilt he had been carrying around for twenty years.

Maggie listened intently to every word. She tried to hold back the tide of tears, but they were soon streaming down her face. She cried for the little boy who had assumed ownership of something so devastating and life altering.

"Declan brought my dad here so he could help me understand things. We finally talked about the night of my mother's death." He shook his head, appearing incredulous. "After all of these years, we finally broke through the wall of silence and dealt with the facts. It wasn't my fault, Maggie. And the truth is, it wasn't my father's fault either. It was an accident. And he's suffered because of it ever since."

"Oh, Finn," Maggie cried out, dabbing at her eyes. "My heart breaks for what your family has endured. I'm so thankful you can put this to rest."

"Me too. I don't know how to put it into words, but my soul feels lighter."

"God is good," Maggie said. "It's amazing, isn't it?"

"For some reason, I always had God in my life. No matter how bad things were, I knew He always walked with me. It prevented me from giving in to total despair. It kept me putting one foot in front of the other and moving forward."

"Oh, Finn. I love you so much. I love your strength

and how you lead with love. Despite the pain you've been dealing with, you always treat others with so much grace. You've been courageous this whole time. And incredibly selfless."

Finn ran his palm over her cheek. "Maggie, you make it so very easy to adore you. I can't imagine a life without you and Oliver in it. And I know God sent you back here so we could fall in love. Just in time for Christmas."

"Oh, Finn. This feels like a dream. I never thought God would bless me twice in a lifetime. I truly loved my husband, but our life together wasn't very happy. For a long time I was angry at him, but I've come to realize his problems were so deep-rooted he couldn't fix them. I feel so blessed to be loved by you and to love you in return."

"I thought I would be walking by myself through life. For so long I didn't think I deserved anything wonderful. I thought my mother's death fell on my shoulders. I came from a family that didn't discuss our pain. We never really talked about how my mother died. We were all just stumbling around trying to make sense of it and stuffing down the pain."

Maggie nodded. "It was such a tragic loss. But it was an accident. None of us are perfect people, but that's the beauty of being loved by God. His love is perfect, so we don't need to be."

"Yes. You're right," Finn said with a nod. "I think the grief for my mother led me to feel as if I was responsible. We lived in a house where things were left unspoken. My mother was the one who bridged those gaps and without her everything fell apart. A mother is truly the heart of a home. It's made me realize how important it is not to keep secrets."

Maggie grazed her hand across Finn's cheek. "I'm so sorry you blamed yourself for all of these years."

"I truly thought the blame was on my shoulders. And I believed if I told anyone, I'd lose everyone I cared about. So I stayed silent over the years. And it was slowly eating me up inside."

"You make a great point about secrets. I've known for a long time now that keeping this secret about the circumstances of Sam's death isn't right. It's weighing me down. In order to move forward I need to be honest about the past. And it might cause Oliver pain, but I have to find a way to tell him the truth. Maybe not today or tomorrow, but somewhere down the line I will." She took a steadying breath. "I think he's resilient enough to deal with it."

"That's why I reacted the way I did when you told me about Sam. I retreated. How could I risk hurting you and Oliver after finding out how badly you'd been wounded by Sam's flaws? That was the reason I never wanted a family of my own. I didn't trust myself not to royally mess everything up."

"Finn, you're not going to mess anything up. I hope you fully realize how strong and loving you are. The love you've shown me and Oliver demonstrates the strength of your heart. Never lose sight of it. It's the very core of who you are."

"From the moment you came back to Love, I knew my heart was shifting." He placed his hand over his heart. "I could feel it. But it scared me. It's frightening to believe you're going to hurt the very people you love the most. You and Oliver are my touchstones. Without you, my life would be a dull shade of gray. With the two of you in it, it pops with color. You make the ordinary things feel extraordinary."

"Oh, Finn. That's beautiful. We came to Love for a fresh start and a new life. From the very start you felt like family to us. I kept worrying about Oliver becoming too attached to you, but he knew right from the start we belonged together."

"Smart kid," Finn said with a chuckle. "He was right all along, wasn't he?"

"He sure was," Maggie said, grabbing Finn by the collar and pulling him toward her so she could place a triumphant kiss on his lips.

"Where are you taking me?" Maggie asked as she peered out the window of Finn's truck. Snow was gently falling past her window. She grinned as she spotted moose-crossing signs. It was now run-of-the-mill to see these signs, and on the rare occasion, she'd actually seen a moose or two crossing the road. She had settled in to her life in this heartwarming town and she loved experiencing everything the town of Love had to offer. Not a day went by that she didn't take the time to thank God and Uncle Tobias for blessing her so abundantly.

"I wanted us to have some alone time," Finn said, turning his gaze away from the road to wink at her.

"Keep your eyes on the road, hotshot," Maggie said

with a laugh, moving closer to Finn so she could snuggle against him.

"We're almost there. Right down this road." Finn expertly navigated his truck down the road heavily packed with snow. A sign announcing the Nottingham Woods came into view. He drove down the lane and pulled his car into the lot. They both got out and began walking toward the forested area, hand in hand.

"I thought it would be nice to bring you to a place where my parents used to take Declan and me when were kids. Did you know they met each other around the same age as we did? They were kids themselves."

"No, Finn. I don't think you ever told me that before." She smiled. "That's really sweet. They were a real love story."

"Just like we are," Finn said, lowering his head and placing a sweet kiss on Maggie's cold lips. Her nose was tingling with cold due to the frigid weather.

Her lips began chattering. She wrapped her arms around herself. "Finn, it's super cold outside. Can we head back to town soon? I'm dreaming of sipping a peppermint hot chocolate at the Moose Café before opening up the shop."

"Hold on for a few minutes, beautiful. I've got something to say." He reached out for her mittened hands and entwined them with his own. "Maggie, I know this might seem fast, but in some ways I think we've known each other for a lifetime. We were best friends when we were ten years old and we still are. I think we both know the importance of seizing the day. Tomorrow isn't promised." He sucked in a huge breath. "I love you, Maggie."

Finn quickly lowered himself to one knee in the snow. He looked up at her with love emanating from his eyes. Maggie felt out of breath. Time seemed to stand still as she watched Finn reach into his jacket pocket and pull out a wooden box.

Finn popped the lid open to reveal a sparkling solitaire diamond surrounded on either side by smaller emeralds. They were the same color as her eyes. Maggie let out a squeal then covered her mouth with her mittened hands. She locked gazes with Finn and let out a sob as she saw the love shining forth in his eyes. "Will you marry me, Maggie? I honestly never thought those words would ever come out of my mouth. I was convinced I'd live out my days alone. Until you. Until Oliver. You made me want to face the past and become a better man. You inspired me to believe I was worthy of happiness."

"Oh, Finn, of course I'll marry you. I adore you. I always have. And you deserve a happy ending more than anyone I know. I'm so blessed you chose me to be a part of it."

Maggie pulled Finn to his feet and helped him brush the snow off his pants.

Maggie continued. "When we were kids you always pushed me out of my comfort zone. And ever since I came back to Love, you've been encouraging me to be more courageous in my life. Your bravery has inspired me. You laid your soul bare about your past and your feelings of guilt. In doing so, you set me free, Finn. You made me realize how I needed to deal with my own issues. And I'll always be thankful for it. My heart is filled to overflowing. I never dared to dream about finding my happy ending. Honestly, I never imagined finding a spouse here in Love. I didn't want one. I was focused on Oliver and wanting his happiness to come first."

He reached for her chin and tilted it up so he could look into her eyes. "You're a wonderful mother, Maggie. You deserve to be happy, and I am so blessed to be the man who gets to spend the rest of his days at your side."

Maggie grinned. "When I left Massachusetts to come to Love, I promised myself two things. I would make a wonderful life here in Alaska for Oliver. And I would be brave. I think I've managed to achieve both of my goals."

"Yes, you have, my love. I'm very proud of you. We're going to have a wonderful life," he promised. He dipped his head down and placed his lips over Maggie's in a tender and triumphant kiss. The kiss celebrated their love and the bright future awaiting them.

"What do you think Oliver will say?" Finn asked. "Do you think he'll be all right with sharing his mother with me?"

Maggie threw her head back and laughed. "Are you kidding? He'll be shouting the news from the rooftops." At the thought of it, Maggie felt tears pool in her eyes. "He loves you just as much as I do. That little boy came to Alaska with a mission. To find a father. I wasn't sure I could give him what he was looking for because even though I tried to be sensitive to his needs, I never really wanted or intended to open up my heart again."

"I'm so glad you changed your mind about that," Finn said in a teasing voice.

"How could I resist the devastatingly charming Finn O'Rourke?" Maggie asked.

Finn reached out and grabbed Maggie by the waist and twirled her around. "I can't wait to tell Oliver his mission has been accomplished," he called out. "I'm going to be the best husband and father in all of Alaska. You've got my word on that."

Maggie reached up and tugged Finn by the collar so she could place a kiss on his lips. "You've already got it in the bag, O'Rourke. What a merry Christmas this will be."

"It sure will." Finn nuzzled his nose against Maggie's and looked deeply into her eyes. "Merry Christmas, my love."

Epilogue

Christmas Day

A feeling of utter peace swept over Maggie. She didn't feel even a hint of anxiety. Her emotions were as calm as a lake in summer. Today promised to be one of the most wonderful days of her life. She was going to become Mrs. Finn O'Rourke. It was the most precious Christmas gift of all. Maggie was prepared to pledge eternity to her childhood best friend and soul mate.

The best things in life came to fruition when you trusted in God's plan and gave your heart wholeheartedly to another human being. With love, faith and trust, anything was possible.

Thank You, Lord, for seeing me through the storms of life. And for pointing me toward the rainbows. Finn is my happily-ever-after, the one I'd stopped hoping for. And he's going to be the best father in the world to Oliver. Thank You for blessing all three of us.

As she sat at her vanity table, Maggie surveyed herself in the mirror. She had always dreamed of getting married in a beautiful ivory gown. It was stunning! She felt elegant and graceful. Since her first marriage had taken place at city hall, this was a real dream come true. A happily-ever-after moment.

A knocking sound at the door drew her attention away from her thoughts.

"Come in," she called out.

The door slowly opened. Her son stood there with a huge grin on his face dressed to the nines in his miniature black tux with the red bow tie.

"Oliver! You look so incredibly handsome." Pride burst inside her chest at the sight of him. Although she had promised herself no crying today, the sight of Oliver threatened her composure. Tears were misting in her eyes.

"Thanks, Mom. And you look like a movie star, only prettier." Oliver had one of his hands behind his back. "I have something for you."

"What is it?"

"I made it myself." Oliver pulled his arm from behind his back and held up a drawing. Maggie let out a gasp. It was a picture of a man, a woman and a little boy.

Oliver pointed to the picture and said, "This is me. And you and Finn. A family."

"Oh, Oliver. It's beautiful." She sniffed away tears. "My loving, creative son."

Maggie held open her arms. Oliver ran into them and hugged her.

"I want you to know, Oliver, how much I love you. Marrying Finn won't ever change the way I feel about you. We're going to be a family. I don't want you to ever forget your father. But I also want you to know that Finn wants to be your forever dad. He loves you so very much." Tears pooled in Maggie's eyes.

"I love him too, Mom. Thank you for bringing us here and for finding Finn. I won't forget Daddy, but I don't think he would mind me loving Finn and having a new dad since he's in Heaven now."

Maggie brushed tears away from her cheeks. "No, baby. He wouldn't mind one little bit. Matter-of-fact, I think he'd be really happy about it." For so long now, Maggie had been mad at Sam. Now, she had come to terms with her former husband's imperfections and his tragic death. In order to embrace her future with Finn, Maggie knew it was important to close the door on her past. Forgiveness was part of the journey.

A short while later she arrived at the church with Hazel, Ruby and Oliver at her side. She watched as her friends walked side by side toward the altar. When the wedding march began to play, Oliver looped his arm through hers, ready to walk her down the aisle toward the love of her life.

"Ready?" Oliver asked, his eyes twinkling as he looked over at her.

Maggie nodded, too overwhelmed with emotion to speak. They began to walk down the aisle strewed with forget-me-nots. She teared up as they walked past a multitude of smiling, supportive faces. There was no doubt in her mind about being a part of this community. The townsfolk of Love had accepted her and Oliver with open arms.

Jasper winked at her as she walked by. Aidan gave Oliver a thumbs-up as they marched by his pew. Dwight beamed at her from his aisle seat.

When they reached the altar, Finn was standing there looking swoon worthy in a black tuxedo and crisp white shirt. A red bow tie and cummerbund gave him a bit of holiday flair. Declan stood at his side. Finn reached out and took Maggie's hand, then raised it to his lips.

"You look breathtaking," he said in a low voice.

"Right back atcha," Maggie said, fighting back tears.

Oliver turned away from them to head toward the front pew.

"Wait, Oliver. I have something for you," Finn said. He reached into his tuxedo pocket and pulled out a scroll tied with a navy blue ribbon.

"For me?" Oliver asked, his face full of surprise.

"Yes," Finn said with a nod. "It's a proclamation from the town of Love that we're one big family. Mayor Jasper signed it, so it's official. I want you to be my son in every way possible. If it's okay with you, your mother and I want you to be Oliver O'Rourke. I want to officially adopt you."

"Really?" Oliver asked with a sob. He swiped at his eyes as tears overflowed his lids. "That means we'll all have the same last name."

Finn took him in his arms and reassured him. "Forever and always, Oliver. Just say the word and we'll get the paperwork started."

"How about today?" Oliver asked, causing a chorus of laughter to erupt in the church.

Finn reached out and tousled his hair, a huge grin

etched on his face. "It's Christmas, Oliver. I'm pretty sure the office is closed today, but tomorrow, bright and early, I'll get the ball rolling."

Oliver smiled and clutched the scroll to his chest, then made his way to the front pew where he sat down next to Ruby, Liam and Aidan.

Pastor Jack faced the congregation and said, "Welcome to this celebration of a mighty love. Finn and Maggie met as children right here in Love." Pastor Jack let out a chuckle. "As they say, God works in mysterious ways. Delight thyself also in the Lord; And He shall give thee the desires of thine heart. God has been good to this couple. He has given them the most fervent desires of their hearts." He nodded toward Finn. "I think Finn has a few words for his bride."

Finn reached out and joined hands with Maggie. "Before you came back I was doing okay. I was getting by. It didn't take me long to figure out you held the key to my future happiness. You brought out something in me I'd buried a long time ago. I was holding on to a heavy burden that weighed me down. Because of you, I was able to face the past and put it in perspective. I was able to break through my pain and embrace true, enduring love. Maggie, being loved by you humbles me. I will love you and Oliver until the end of my days."

Maggie reached out and wiped away the tears streaming down Finn's face.

She looked deeply into his eyes as she spoke. "I came to Love to start fresh and to build a solid foundation for Oliver. I never imagined I would find a love of a lifetime. Finn—you and Oliver are my world. I promise never to forsake you. I'll be by your side, no matter what challenges we might face."

As the ceremony continued, Pastor Jack pronounced Finn and Maggie as husband and wife. Finn dipped his head down and placed a tender kiss on his beloved's lips. Joy filled the small church as the guests began to clap thunderously.

Finn and Maggie, with Oliver right by their side, walked down the aisle and out of the church into the brilliant December afternoon. Oliver reached into his pocket and began to throw red rose petals at his parents. Laughter filled the air.

Life was just beginning. And the world was their oyster.

* * * * *

If you enjoyed this book, look for the other books in the ALASKAN GROOMS *series:*

AN ALASKAN WEDDING
ALASKAN REUNION
A MATCH MADE IN ALASKA
REUNITED AT CHRISTMAS
HIS SECRET ALASKAN HEIRESS

Available now from Love Inspired!

Find more great reads at www.LoveInspired.com

Dear Reader,

Thank you for joining me on another Alaskan love story. I hope you enjoyed *An Alaskan Christmas*. There's something so wonderful about the Christmas season. It's truly a time to draw closer to your loved ones, celebrate the birth of Jesus and enjoy the sights and smells of the holiday. Eggnog! Sugar cookies. A deliciously baked ham. One of my favorite things to do during the holiday season is to drive around with my family looking at Christmas lights and decorations. It's a feast for the eyes.

Finn and Maggie share a precious bond as childhood friends. Although it's been twenty years since they've seen each other, they quickly fall into the familiar rhythms of their friendship. Ever since I introduced Finn in *A Match Made in Alaska* I've been thinking about him and what makes him tick. Why was he always running away from Love, as well as running from love? And could Maggie find love again, even though she thinks she's done with romance? Somehow, through God's divine grace, he and Maggie find their happily-ever-after in each other's arms.

It's always a treat for me to hear from readers. I can be reached by email at scalhoune@gmail.com. I can also be found on my Author Belle Calhoune Facebook page, on my website, bellecalhoune.com, or on Twitter @BelleCalhoune.

Blessings,
Belle

COMING NEXT MONTH FROM
Love Inspired®

Available October 17, 2017

SECRET CHRISTMAS TWINS
Christmas Twins • by Lee Tobin McClain

Erica Lindholm never expected her Christmas gift would be becoming guardian to twin babies! But fulfilling her promise to keep their parentage a secret becomes increasingly difficult when her holiday plans mean spending time with—and falling for—their uncle, Jason Stephanidis, on the family farm.

AN AMISH PROPOSAL
Amish Hearts • by Jo Ann Brown

Pregnant and without options, Katie Kay Lapp is grateful when past love Micah Stoltzfus helps her find a place to stay. But when he proposes a marriage of convenience, she refuses. Because Katie Kay wants much more—she wants the heart of the man she once let go.

CHRISTMAS ON THE RANCH
by Arlene James and Lois Richer

Spend Christmas with two handsome ranchers in these two brand-new holiday novellas, where a stranger's joyful spirit provides healing for one bachelor, and a single mom with a scarred past is charmed by her little girl's wish for a cowboy daddy.

THE COWBOY'S FAMILY CHRISTMAS
Cowboys of Cedar Ridge • by Carolyne Aarsen

Returning to the Bar W Ranch, Reuben Walsh finds his late brother's widow, Leanne, fighting to keep the place running. Reuben's committed to helping out while he's around—even if it means spending time with the woman who once broke his heart. Can they come to an agreement—and find a happily-ever-after in time for the holidays?

THE LAWMAN'S YULETIDE BABY
Grace Haven • by Ruth Logan Herne

Having a baby dropped on his doorstep changes everything for state trooper Gabe Cutter. After asking widowed single mom next door Corinne Gallagher for help, he's suddenly surrounded by the lights, music and holiday festivities he's avoided for years. This Christmas, can they put their troubled pasts behind and create a family together?

A TEXAS HOLIDAY REUNION
Texas Cowboys • by Shannon Taylor Vannatter

After his father volunteers Colson Kincaid to help at Resa McCall's ranch over Christmas, the single dad is reunited with his old love. Colson's used to managing horses, but can he keep his feelings for Resa from spilling over—and from revealing a truth about his daughter's parentage that could devastate them forever?

LOOK FOR THESE AND OTHER LOVE INSPIRED BOOKS WHEREVER BOOKS ARE SOLD, INCLUDING MOST BOOKSTORES, SUPERMARKETS, DISCOUNT STORES AND DRUGSTORES.

LICNM1017

Get 2 Free Books,
Plus 2 Free Gifts—
just for trying the
Reader Service!

Love Inspired®

YES! Please send me 2 FREE Love Inspired® Romance novels and my 2 FREE mystery gifts (gifts are worth about $10 retail). After receiving them, if I don't wish to receive any more books, I can return the shipping statement marked "cancel." If I don't cancel, I will receive 6 brand-new novels every month and be billed just $5.24 for the regular-print edition or $5.74 each for the larger-print edition in the U.S., or $5.74 each for the regular-print edition or $6.24 each for the larger-print edition in Canada. That's a saving of at least 13% off the cover price. It's quite a bargain! Shipping and handling is just 50¢ per book in the U.S. and 75¢ per book in Canada.* I understand that accepting the 2 free books and gifts places me under no obligation to buy anything. I can always return a shipment and cancel at any time. The free books and gifts are mine to keep no matter what I decide.

Please check one:

☐ Love Inspired Romance Regular-Print
(105/305 IDN GLWW)

☐ Love Inspired Romance Larger-Print
(122/322 IDN GLWW)

Name _____ (PLEASE PRINT)

Address _____ Apt. #

City _____ State/Province _____ Zip/Postal Code

Signature (if under 18, a parent or guardian must sign)

Mail to the **Reader Service:**
IN U.S.A.: P.O. Box 1341, Buffalo, NY 14240-8531
IN CANADA: P.O. Box 603, Fort Erie, Ontario L2A 5X3

Want to try two free books from another line?
Call 1-800-873-8635 today or visit www.ReaderService.com.

*Terms and prices subject to change without notice. Prices do not include applicable taxes. Sales tax applicable in N.Y. Canadian residents will be charged applicable taxes. Offer not valid in Quebec. This offer is limited to one order per household. Books received may not be as shown. Not valid for current subscribers to Love Inspired Romance books. All orders subject to approval. Credit or debit balances in a customer's account(s) may be offset by any other outstanding balance owed by or to the customer. Please allow 4 to 6 weeks for delivery. Offer available while quantities last.

Your Privacy—The Reader Service is committed to protecting your privacy. Our Privacy Policy is available online at www.ReaderService.com or upon request from the Reader Service.

We make a portion of our mailing list available to reputable third parties that offer products we believe may interest you. If you prefer that we not exchange your name with third parties, or if you wish to clarify or modify your communication preferences, please visit us at www.ReaderService.com/consumerschoice or write to us at Reader Service Preference Service, P.O. Box 9062, Buffalo, NY 14240-9062. Include your complete name and address.

LI17R2

SPECIAL EXCERPT FROM

Love Inspired®

*When Erica Lindholm and her twin babies show up at
his family farm just before Christmas, Jason Stephanidis
can tell she's hiding something. But how can he refuse
the young mother, a friend of his sister's, a place to stay
during the holidays? He never counted on wanting Erica
and the boys to be a more permanent part of his life…*

Read on for a sneak peek of
SECRET CHRISTMAS TWINS
by *Lee Tobin McClain*,
part of the **CHRISTMAS TWINS** miniseries.

Once both twins were bundled, snug between Papa
and Erica, Jason sent the horses trotting forward.
The sun was up now, making millions of diamonds
on the snow that stretched across the hills far into
the distance. He smelled pine, a sharp, resin-laden
sweetness.

When he picked up the pace, the sleigh bells jingled.

"Real sleigh bells!" Erica said, and then, as they
approached the white covered bridge decorated with a
simple wreath for Christmas, she gasped. "This is the
most beautiful place I've ever seen."

Jason glanced back, unable to resist watching her fall
in love with his home.

Papa was smiling for the first time since he'd learned
of Kimmie's death. And as they crossed the bridge and
trotted toward the church, converging with other horse-
drawn sleighs, Jason felt a sense of rightness.

Mikey started babbling to Teddy, accompanied by gestures and much repetition of his new word. Teddy tilted his head to one side and burst forth with his own stream of nonsense syllables, seeming to ask a question, batting Mikey on the arm. Mikey waved toward the horses and jabbered some more, as if he were explaining something important.

They were such personalities, even as little as they were. Jason couldn't help smiling as he watched them interact.

Once Papa had the reins set and the horses tied up, Jason jumped out of the sleigh, and then turned to help Erica down. She handed him a twin. "Can you hold Mikey?"

He caught a whiff of baby powder and pulled the little one tight against his shoulder. Then he reached out to help Erica, and she took his hand to climb down, Teddy on her hip.

When he held her hand, something electric seemed to travel right to his heart. Involuntarily he squeezed and held on.

She drew in a sharp breath as she looked at him, some mixture of puzzlement and awareness in her eyes.

What was Erica's secret?

And wasn't it curious that, after all these years, there were twins in the farmhouse again?

Don't miss
SECRET CHRISTMAS TWINS
by Lee Tobin McClain, available November 2017
wherever Love Inspired® books and ebooks are sold.

www.LoveInspired.com

Copyright © 2017 Harlequin Books S.A.

LIEXP1017

Join *USA TODAY* bestselling author

SHEILA ROBERTS

for the final installment in her treasured Icicle Falls series.

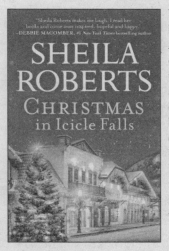

When Muriel Sterling released her new book, *A Guide to Happy Holidays*, she felt like the queen of Christmas. She's thrilled when the new tree she ordered online arrives and is eager to show it off—until she gets it out of the box and realizes it's a mangy dud. But Muriel decides to make it a project, realizing there's a lesson to be learned: everything and everyone has potential. Maybe even her old friend Arnie, who's loved her for years...

Meanwhile, Muriel's ugly-tree project has also inspired her friends. Sienna Moreno is trying to bring out the best in the grouchy man next door. And while Olivia Claussen would love to send her obnoxious new daughter-in-law packing, she's adjusting her attitude and trying to discover what her son sees in the girl. If these women can learn to see the beauty in the "ugly trees" in their lives, perhaps this might turn out to be the happiest holiday yet.

Available October 24, wherever books are sold!

Be sure to connect with us at:
Harlequin.com/Newsletters
Facebook.com/HarlequinBooks
Twitter.com/HarlequinBooks

mira

Harlequin.com

MSR3079